Buoys & Girls

DREAMBOAT CRUISES
BOOK ONE

CYNTHIA GUNDERSON

Dedication

For lovers of long stories made short.

With Gratitude

Editing and Critique
Scott Gunderson

Cover Design
100 Covers

Assistants and Sanity Support
Kyra Schroeder, Desri Wulandari

Chapter One

The first thing I see when we step out of the Uber is a wall of southern Florida humanity. Skin. Suitcases. Roller bags. A kid dragging a stuffed flamingo by one limp leg.

So much skin.

I'm jealous since I chose to wear a sweater and leggings so I wouldn't freeze on the plane, but now I'm sweating like I stole something. I'm also hoping that kid isn't bunking next to me on the cruise ship since he's now screaming bloody murder because he dropped the flamingo.

"Welcome to the cattle drive." Tori hikes her backpack higher on her shoulder. She's got her blond bob tucked under a baseball cap, with her guns out. She's a rock climber, and it shows.

"I dare you to moo," Jamie says, and I guffaw. A red-eye flight plus a donut for breakfast means I'm midnight delirious.

We join the line snaking toward the terminal doors. The air in Miami feels like walking into someone's mouth. Hot, humid, and a little sour, which is probably due to the trash cans on our left. The tank top under my sweater clings to my spine. I would take off the sweater, but I'm not wearing a bra. My second rule of plane survival. Let the girls breathe.

Jamie bumps her shoulder against mine, eyes shining. "Do you think if we don't get on the ship, I won't turn thirty?"

She's the reason we all made the trek to be here. Five foot nothing, brown skin glowing even after no shower, curls piled on top of her head. She's wearing white shorts and a yellow crop top with "Thirty, Flirty, and Cruising" in glitter across the front. It's so cute, I don't even care that it doesn't rhyme.

"You already turned thirty last Friday," Chloe quips, tucking a piece of her long dark hair behind one ear as she maneuvers her suitcase around a pothole. She's in a breezy blue sundress that makes her look like she belongs in a travel brochure.

Jamie snorts. None of us had much sleep last night since we all flew from somewhere in the western US, and it shows.

"Okay, did everyone get some memo I didn't?" I point to their outfits, then to mine.

"Babe, didn't you change when you got off the plane?" Tori gives me a pitying look as we slow and then stop at the back of the line.

Honestly, never occurred to me. I blow out a resigned breath, and Nina laughs. "I'm sure there will be a bathroom in there."

"Probably gross, though." Chloe gives me a look.

Jamie scoffs. "Okay, better attitudes, please? This is happy vibes only. From this point on." She draws a theoretical line on the pavement.

I shift my grip on my duffel and roll my suitcase forward another inch as the line lurches. Ahead of us, the white hull of the Dreamboat Aria rises out of the water like a skyscraper on its side, gleaming in the early afternoon sun. It's their newest ship. I stalked promotional videos like they were my high-school crush. Glass elevators, infinity pools, a rooftop jogging track with ocean views. When they announced this itinerary—Miami to Key West, Cozumel, Belize City, then Dreamboat's private island before looping back—I was the first one dropping links in our group chat.

"It's a miracle we made it," Chloe says. *Well, most of us.* She continues, "Nobody got fired. Or pregnant."

Tori laughs out loud. "Okay, that's a low blow."

Tori ruined our attempts at a summer trip to Catalina Island with a pregnancy scare. When it turned out to be a false alarm, none of us could decide if we were relieved or disappointed.

Behind us, Nina turns in a slow circle, her long copper hair floating like she's Ariel. Her tall and willowy physique and green romper only solidify the comparison, though the aviators pushed up on her head make her almost human.

She lifts her phone, filming a slow pan of the line and the ship. "Content, ladies. I expect you all to contribute."

Chloe rolls her eyes. "There's a reason I didn't sign up for the data plan. My phone is going in the safe and not coming out until next weekend."

Jamie scoffs. "Then how are we going to communicate?"

"I have a roommate." Chloe flashes a smile.

If only I had her self-control. Not that I think my business will die while I'm gone, but if there's an issue, I need to be available. I don't see many true emergencies as a physical therapist, but I love my patients. And since I moved back to Billings two years ago, I've been steadily growing my client base.

This trip is the first time in, I don't even know how long, when my schedule isn't measured in thirty-minute increments and an endless list of insurance codes. It makes me a little nervous.

Seven days. Four ports. No charts, no notes. Most importantly, no ex-boyfriend leaving his hockey gear in my front hall like a mildew bomb. I didn't move back to Montana for him.

But I didn't *not* move back because of him. It had been six months since we called it quits, but every time I saw his truck in town, it felt like it had only been weeks.

The line shuffles forward. Loudspeaker announcements echo off the concrete overhead. Families try to keep kids corralled. A group of college guys starts an off-key rendition of "Sweet Caroline" in the distance. Promising.

I wasn't pining in the least for my ex. But I wouldn't have stayed with him for so long if I didn't love the companionship. That person to go home to. I was barely getting to the point where I wouldn't score a ten out of ten on the loneliness scale of a mental health survey.

My phone buzzes in my back pocket.

I pull it out, already knowing who it is.

MEL:

Send pics

I laugh and text back:

You ditched us, remember?

MEL:

Staaaahp. You know I didn't have a choice

I tilt my phone screen so the others can see, then hit the voice memo button. We fill the audio with "Miss you!" and a few "Boo"s.

Mel will absolutely be missed, but she had the chance of a lifetime to acquire a new marketing company. It's going to be huge for her, and none of us resent the choice. Of anyone, I had the right to be the most pissed because she was supposed to be my cabin mate.

Secretly? I'm a little excited to have the room to myself. That way I can get my work in without attracting the "unplug" comments. Plus, those bathrooms are smaller than my shower back at home.

I'll miss her, but it's the best of both our worlds. Especially since we've already made plans to meet in San Diego for her thirtieth birthday in March.

ME:

> Work can suck it
>
> Also, the private balcony makes me less mad

A new series of crying emojis comes through, followed by:

MEL:

> Put that bed to good use on my behalf

I send a laughing emoji and a heart, then slip my phone back into my purse before Chloe can notice and give me a dirty look.

Ten minutes later, we finally reach the terminal doors and shuffle inside. Air conditioning hits my face, and I audibly sigh. After checking our suitcases, we're guided up an escalator into a large waiting hall with check-in counters along one side, rows of chairs, and digital screens listing boarding groups.

"Okay." I scan the options. "We checked in online. We should be Group . . . three?"

"Group three, baby." Tori points at a screen where the words "Now Boarding: Group 2" flash.

We join the cluster of people near the Group 3 sign. I dig out my passport and pull up the boarding information on my phone.

I can't believe it's been three years of friendship between the six of us. I'll be honest, the reason I joined a beginner boxing class at the rec center wasn't to meet other women. Wink, wink. But it's by far the best thing to come from that class. Well, besides my right hook.

The first night, I'd walked into that fluorescent-lit room in my old college soccer shorts and a tank top. Jamie was there because a client at the marketing firm she worked for had given her a free pass. Nina had signed up to support one of her photography buddies. Chloe had come to support Jamie after a bad breakup.

There were only two men in the class, and none of us paid them any attention because we instantly clicked. We were all equally terrible at punching, footwork, and pivoting. But we laughed. A lot.

There's a specific intimacy that forms when you've accidentally punched someone in the boob three weeks in a row. We started grabbing smoothies after class, then brunch, then movie nights. When the boxing class ended, the group chat didn't.

When Jamie turned twenty-nine last year and said she wanted to do something "epic" for thirty, this cruise became the answer.

"Group three, you are now boarding at Gate C," a staff member calls over the speaker.

The group of guys ahead of us cheers.

Tori frowns. "Do guys go on . . . big group guy vacations?"

Nina considers this. "Maybe it's a team or something." Her eyes widen. "Maybe it's a hockey team?"

Chloe gives me a look. "Don't even start."

"It's true," I say. "Those hot hockey players aren't all they're cracked up to be."

Jamie shakes her head as the line starts to move. "Just because you got a douchebag doesn't mean they're all that way. And . . ." She spins toward us, her face making an "I'm sorry, but also super excited about something" expression.

"Oh no," Chloe mutters.

"I might've chosen this week for a reason."

I stare at her blankly. "What do you mean?"

She bites her lower lip. "I found out that—"

"The line's moving," a man grunts from behind us.

Chloe's eyes flash as Jamie apologizes and holds up a hand. I love both of them for that. We scoot forward as Jamie talks over her shoulder.

"I found out that this week is kind of a singles week on the ship."

"Say what now?" Tori raises an eyebrow.

"A single's week. Like, where they have all these mixers and—"

"Are we signed up for that shit?" Chloe squeaks.

Jamie's face squinches. "Just a little?"

The group of guys now scanning in and receiving their wristbands makes a lot more sense.

Nina laughs out loud. Tori blinks. And I?

A flurry of emotion swirls in my chest. Disappointment because the last thing I want to think about is men or dating. This whole trip was supposed to be just us. Preemptive exhaustion because meeting new people, while exciting and fun in my twenties, now sounds about as fun as getting blood-work done.

Jamie and Nina are the hopeful, glass-half-full members of our group. Chloe is usually glass-is-empty, and Tori and I are more why-are-we-thinking-about-the-glass?

But it is Jamie's birthday. We're here for her, and she's still a hopeless romantic. I've also never been more grateful to have my own cabin. It's not hard to fake nausea or vertigo on a ship. I grin smugly to myself, knowing that while the rest of them will have to come up with real excuses to skip evening singles activities, I'll be home free.

We shuffle forward, and Chloe gives me a look that says she knows exactly what I'm thinking. I fight back a smile because she's rooming with Jamie.

"Okay, but I don't get the point of this," Tori says. "We meet guys from all over the country, get to know them, and then what? Get off the ship? No way that works long term."

That's my girl.

Nina scoffs. "You wouldn't move if you found the guy of your dreams?" She nudges Jamie. "I think it's a great idea, by the way."

"Right?" Jamie gives us all chastising looks. "Who doesn't want a romance at sea?"

I start to raise my hand, but Nina grabs it with a laugh.

Jamie sobers. "I promise, we'll still do all girl stuff. We don't have to do everything. I just thought it would be fun to dress up, choose from a few events, and hang out with other single people. Not just men."

When she puts it that way, it doesn't sound like the worst. "As long as I get time with my girls, I'm happy." I pull Nina and Chloe in, and they both grab Tori and Jamie for an impromptu group hug.

When the guy behind us mutters again, we break apart and move with the herd onto the gangway. Once we've scanned and received our bands, we're on the deck and then walking through sliding glass doors onto the ship.

The entrance to the Dreamboat Aria is like stepping into a movie set. The atrium opens up in front of us, soaring up several decks. Glass-sided elevators glide silently past glittering light fixtures. The floor gleams, pale marble veined with gold. There's a grand staircase sweeping upward, flanked by potted palms and a tourmaline sculpture that looks like a wave frozen in midair.

"It smells like Dior," Nina says. She's not wrong.

People mill around. A few families and couples, but more groups of friends that look like us. Crew members in crisp navy uniforms smile and direct traffic.

"It's like the Titanic," Chloe says. "You know. Before."

"Wow, love that energy," I say. "Thank you for that."

"Like, minus the iceberg, plus OSHA."

I snort.

"Where do we go?" Jamie's head is swiveling like an owl.

Tori takes charge, looking at the map and ushering us to our checkpoint. I'm beyond thrilled that they aren't doing any emergency drill with life jackets. When we're finished, we still have an hour to kill before our cabins are ready, so we opt for food.

When we're sufficiently stuffed and relaxed, courtesy of the welcome mimosas, we take the elevator down to deck five, following the hallway signs toward our section. The carpet is patterned in swirling blues and golds, and doors with little plaques line the corridor on both sides.

Our cabins are midship. Perfect, so we're close to the stairs. I count off numbers on the doors until we reach the first one in our block.

Jamie squeals, and even Chloe can't help but absorb some of her over-the-top energy. Chloe leans down and checks the tags on the bags, even though the vintage bag with the brass corner protectors is clearly hers.

"Swimsuits? Pool deck?" Jamie asks.

We all nod our heads. Tori and Nina find their bags and open the door to their room, which leaves me in the next one.

I give Chloe a slow wave, then swipe my band over the sensor. Hm. Strange. My bag isn't in the hall. They're probably doing the rooms in batches and maybe—

I gasp. Jumping back and running into the door frame.

There's a man. In this room. He's standing next to the bed wearing board shorts and nothing else. Tan skin, broad shoulders, a line of muscle running from his chest down his stomach. There's a suitcase open on the bed to the right, clothes piled beside it in careful stacks. He holds a folded T-shirt in frozen hands, eyes wide.

"I—I'm so sorry, I—" I turn to leave, fighting with the door and finally escaping back to the hall. My breath comes in fits and spurts.

What the hell?

I lift my wristband, my brain short-circuiting. My band opened the door. *His* band obviously opened the door. But my bag isn't here, so maybe—

The door swings open behind me.

I whirl around so fast my ponytail smacks me in the cheek. The shirtless man stands in the doorway now, holding his folded T-shirt like a shield. His expression is somewhere between apologetic and bewildered.

"Hey," he says carefully. "So. Uh . . ."

Yeah. Exactly. "I'm going to—" I point down the hall, my eyes slipping from his face without permission. I whirl and call back, "I'll find guest services. Just a mix-up, I'm sure."

I march down the hall like I'm escaping a crime scene.

Behind me, his bare feet slap against the carpet as he jogs to catch up.

"What are you—?"

"I'm coming with you," he interrupts, yanking his shirt over his head and pushing his arms through the holes. The shirt slides over his stomach, and it's then that I realize I've stopped.

"Oh. Okay." I blink and force myself to keep walking. That makes sense. He must be just as disturbed as I am that we both had access to the same room.

We make it to the elevators, and when the doors open, I jab the button for deck six, where we entered the ship. It seems like Guest Services would have to be there in that atrium.

The guy from my cabin steps in next to me, giving me a wide berth. His hair is still a little damp, dark brown and curling slightly at the ends. His toes curl against the tile like he's trying to touch it with as little of his body as possible.

"They probably just cleaned it," I say.

"There have been a thousand people on this elevator today. And they all walked through Miami."

That is a fair point. "I could've waited for you to put on shoes."

He raises an eyebrow. Well. Another good argument.

I pull out my phone and check the time. It's only been five minutes, but Jamie seemed motivated to get to the pool. At least we should still be able to text since we haven't left port.

"Are you here with anyone?" he asks as the elevator dings and the doors slide open.

"Just some friends."

"Just?"

"I—friends. My best friends."

We step out into the buzzing atrium on deck six, where a host of newly boarded passengers crowd around the Guest Services desk. There's a line, which is predictable. By the huffs and tapping fingers, it seems to be moving at the pace of a thousand-year-old glacier.

I drag a palm down my face. "This is my personal hell."

"Not a line person?"

I turn. "Nobody's a line person."

He shrugs. "They can be fun. If you're with the right

person." Then he stalks off toward the desk, bypassing the line completely.

It's the first time I see him from the back. He's got nice calves.

He walks up to the far end of the counter and leans over, catching the attention of a woman shuffling through paperwork, not at a computer station. They exchange a few words, then he points in my direction. She nods, then frowns, then disappears into a back room.

My mystery man raises a hand and motions for me to come over. I keep my head down and try to ignore the dirty looks from the other passengers in line.

"What are you doing?" I hiss.

"Asking about the room. Isn't that—?"

"There's a line."

He shrugs. "She was available."

I open my mouth, but before I can get a word out, a man in crisp white slacks and a fitted navy blazer with a gold "Derek" nametag arrives in front of us. He's tall with perfectly groomed dark hair, a smooth tan, and the kind of smile you see on Waterpik commercials.

"Sounds like we're having a room issue?" Derek says, commandeering a computer from another staff member who is wrestling with the printer.

I wet my lips. "Uh, yes. I went to the room I was assigned, but he was already in it."

The man grins. "Mason. Such a scoundrel."

I look between the two of them. "Do you—?"

"I gave her my band," Mason says, motioning at the back room where the staff member he'd been talking to had disappeared.

Derek holds it up as proof, then motions for me to hand him mine. He scans them both and scrolls on his screen.

"Alright, looks like . . ." He frowns, then looks at me. "Did you have someone you were rooming with?"

I nod. "Yes. Her name's Mel Asay, but she won't be checking in. She had a work thing come up."

He nods. "I'm seeing that. She called. But that meant you were reassigned a roommate—"

"I'm sorry, what?"

He turns the computer monitor to face me and points halfway down the screen at a series of check boxes. "You selected the matched roommate option."

I lean closer, trying to process the words in front of me.

"It's something we do for Buoys & Girls Week. Part of our singles programming. You can opt for—"

"No, I hear what you're saying, but I already had a roommate listed in the cabin I booked. I only clicked that because I was saying I had a roommate."

Derek smiles knowingly. "I understand. Unfortunately, that's not what the question is asking. We match solo travelers by age and gender preference—"

"But I'm not a solo traveler."

Mason steps forward. "Right. She's here with her best friends."

"How many of you are there?" Derek asks.

I swallow. "Five. Including me."

He pauses, as if waiting for that to sink in.

"But we paid for the whole cabin," I argue. How could they charge Mel and then give away her spot?

"Your roommate's portion was refunded . . ." He drags out the last word, scanning the screen. "Yep. It was refunded to the credit card on file on January sixth."

My throat bobs. *She was refunded?* I pull out my phone and swipe to my conversation with Mel, trying to find the message she'd sent letting me know she couldn't make it, but the words blur together.

"That's not—I didn't click that box," Mason says, running a hand through his hair. "I have responsibilities that require—"

"Your cruise was booked by corpor—" Derek starts, but Mason cuts him off.

"Yes, my company sent me, but there were specific accommodation requests."

I pause in my scrolling. His company sent him on a solo cruise? My brain spins through potential explanations for that, coming up with a handful. *A workaholic? Health issues? Bereavement?*

Derek shakes his head. "It looks like you were enrolled in the Buoys and Girls programming, including the roommate matching. And same for you, Ms. Carter.

Jamie. I purse my lips.

"You're attending Buoys and Girls?" Mason asks, his eyebrows rising.

My expression pinches. "What? I don't seem like a good candidate?"

"That's not—no, you just seemed—"

"My friend signed us all up. I thought this was a girl's trip," I snap, then draw a breath through my nose. "Sorry. Just a little stressed by all this."

Derek looks between the two of us. "So . . . We're at full capacity. Even if you did want to pay for a single cabin, we don't have availability. Buoys & Girls Week sells out every time."

My stomach drops. "There has to be something."

He scrolls the wheel on the mouse and shakes his head. "The only thing I have is a presidential suite."

"What does that cost?" I ask.

Derek clicks, then clicks again. "Looks like it comes with three bedrooms with private bathrooms, a living area with a wraparound balcony, and—"

"It's twenty thousand," Mason quips.

Derek nods. "Pretty close. Nineteen-five for the week."

My eyes bug out of my head. *Three thousand dollars a night?* How could any room be worth that?

"It comes with a private hot tub and masseuse," Derek says, as if that explains everything.

"I'd have to sell both my kidneys," I mutter, and Mason snorts. My cheeks flush. Hadn't meant to say that out loud.

"Well . . . " Derek tilts his head. "One option is: one of you may disembark—"

"What?!" My blood pressure spikes.

Derek shrugs. "Just presenting the choices."

I inhale slowly. Jamie's thirtieth birthday. A year of planning. Matching outfits. Group chat spreadsheets. I am not—*not*—missing this cruise.

Mason straightens. "No one is disembarking. It's fine. I'm sure we can figure it out."

My mouth opens and closes like a fish. Unless Mason had someone else he was planning to bunk with, there was no figuring this out.

"I'll share," he says, leaning his hip against the countertop. His eyes are fixed on me, his mouth curled at one corner. He's daring me. Forcing me to be the asshole in this situation if I refuse to share a cabin with a complete and total stranger.

My hands go numb. "I'm not going to sleep in a room with someone I know nothing about. You could be a serial killer or—"

"No, we background check everyone who comes on the ship for Buoys and Girls week. Also in your forms," Derek says, planting his palms on the counter.

"Just because someone hasn't murdered yet doesn't mean they won't." I glare at Mason.

He smirks. "I can text you references if you want—"

"Just send your psych evaluations," Derek says. "I'm sure you've had those at work, right?"

Mason's expression slackens.

"Mason here is a paramedic," Derek continues. "Saving lives all over . . ." he checks his screen. "New York City."

My eyebrows shoot up. *New York?* Mason wasn't giving that vibe in the least with his board shorts, T-shirt, and bare feet.

Mason runs a hand over his face, and I swear he says something like, "Thanks, bro," under his breath.

Derek seems pleased with himself. "You were both matched based on your surveys, and since you opted in—"

"I didn't opt in," I correct him.

Derek points at the "Buoys and Girls" label on my details. *Right.*

Truly, if anyone was going to be motivated to take someone's life, it was me.

"So, if nobody's getting off the ship," Derek says brightly, handing us each our bands back, "you're roommates for the week. Congratulations!"

Chapter Three

On the adults-only pool deck, music thumps from hidden speakers, and I have to squint against the sunlight that ricochets off water, glass, and bleached deck chairs. Everywhere I look, there's motion. People laughing, lathering up with sunscreen, and balancing drinks the size of small aquariums.

I spot my friends immediately. They've claimed a cluster of loungers near the main pool, towels spread and damp like they've already been here for hours.

Jamie sees me first and sits bolt upright. "She lives!"

I drop my purse on the closest chair and get pelted with questions.

"Is he hot?"

"What's his name?"

"There were *no* other cabins?"

"Mel got a refund?"

I shouldn't have texted them anything until I got here. Hindsight is 20/20.

I hold up my hands. "His name's Mason. There was only a suite, and it must be laced with gold for how much it costs, and yes. Mel got a refund."

Tori raises an eyebrow. "So he's hot."

I pull off my swim cover. I'd hoped they wouldn't notice I skipped that one. "He's not unattractive."

Chloe smiles with knives. "Oh. He's extremely hot."

"Shut up." A blush hits my cheeks. I try to cover it up by searching through my bag for sunscreen. My stomach is all fluttery, and it makes me lightheaded.

Being alone with Mason in that tiny cabin was disorienting, to say the least. And that was just for the five minutes it took me to change into my swimsuit and freshen up from the flight. Everywhere I went, I could smell his soap or cologne, and if we were both moving, there was a good chance we'd brush arms.

It turned out that my bag was already in the room. Mason had called the staff about that, which meant he at least wasn't a creep who'd planned to search my luggage and steal my underwear or something.

I slather my shoulders in sunscreen, then sink onto the edge of Jamie's chair and press my palms into my eyes. Then I tell them everything. The door. The abs. The mutual horror. Guest Services. Derek at Guest Services, changing into my swimsuit in the bathroom, realizing my cover-up was back in my bag, and being forced to appear half-naked in front of Mason.

Half-naked on the pool deck felt appropriate. In the bedroom with a random dude? That hit different.

"So." Nina pushes her sunglasses up her nose. "You're sharing a cabin with a hot paramedic. I fail to see the disaster here."

Jamie's smile almost reaches the bottom of her Elizabeth Taylor sunglasses. "It's perfect. Who doesn't want a cruise ship fling?"

I scoff. "Maybe Nina wants it! I'm not exactly the fling type."

Nina nods in agreement. I half think about asking her to switch rooms with me, but something about that thought twists between my ribs. I blink. I don't have time to analyze whatever the hell that feeling was because Tori is already launching into logistics.

"You could bunk with us. Don't they have those wall bunk beds? That you pull down from the ceiling or something?"

I picture that tiny room with three women sharing it and shudder. "Absolutely not. I love you all too much to destroy our friendship that way."

Jamie stretches her arms over her head. "Listen. I signed us up for the whole singles thing because we're all getting a little comfortable." Before Chloe can cut in, she continues, "You know it's true. All of us have had bad breakups in the past couple of years, and we need to get over it. I'm thirty, y'all are right there with me. We have good jobs, great bodies, we're smart and funny and ambitious—"

"Yeah. Exactly why we can't find good men," I say. I wish it weren't the truth, but it seems like every guy we've collectively dated has wanted a mom, not a girlfriend.

Jamie pushes her sunglasses up onto her head. "That's exactly why this is a good idea. Any guys on this cruise have had to put forth effort. They had to plan a trip, get their asses on a plane, and pack. They probably have friends in *real life*."

I had to admit. That was a lot of green flags.

"They could just be looking for hook-ups," Chloe says.

Jamie shakes her head. "I'm not going to say that doesn't happen, but I researched this thoroughly. This isn't just a "get drunk with other single people" thing. They have structured programming to help you get to know each other and connect. Men want that as much as women do."

I wanted to believe that was true. But I had yet to see it in the men I'd been romantically involved with.

"The guy you got paired with is doing Buoys and Girls week, right?" Jamie asks me.

I nod. It did seem that way, but I was still confused by our interactions with Derek. Had his work booked him on a hook-up cruise? *What kind of job did he have?*

"Right. So maybe he's just as sick of the dating apps as we are," Jamie continues. "We all know it sucks, so it shouldn't be embarrassing to want to do something different. This week sells out every quarter. I heard they were thinking of making it a monthly thing. It's so popular. And they have a whole page dedicated to the weddings of people who met on their ships." She shrugs, her face saying, "the proof's in the pudding."

Chloe let's out an exasperated sigh. "But I don't wanna."

Nina pets her hair like a cat. "We'll get through this together." She looks up at me. "Except Liv. She'll get through this with Mason."

I grab one of the stacked towels on the chair next to me and chuck it at her.

Chapter Four

The opening mixer for Buoys & Girls is in a lounge that feels explicitly designed for foreplay. Low lighting, faux candles, and cocktails with names like *Port of Call Me*. People cluster in loose groups, their name tags crookedly pinned to shirt pockets and dress straps.

We enter together, but Jamie is immediately pulled into deep conversation with two women in front of the drink station. Tori starts flirting with a guy built like a refrigerator, who straight up turns and introduces himself, leaving me, Chloe, and Nina wallflowering.

It doesn't take long for me to spot him.

Mason stands near the bar, hands in his pockets. He's changed into a long-sleeved button-down, sleeves rolled just enough to show forearms that might be nicer than his calves, which are thankfully hidden under linen pants. He's not talking to anyone, but he looks content. Not on his phone. Just observing.

It's unnerving.

"That's him?" Nina asks, following my line of attention.

I clear my throat and turn to stare out the pitch black

windows. We left port a couple of hours ago, and the coast has long since faded behind us. "That's him."

Chloe gives a smug smile. "He's not talking to anyone. Is he waiting for you?"

"Stop." There's a pang I don't expect. Pity, maybe? He doesn't look lonely, but at no point did Mason mention friends he was meeting up with. And the whole work thing . . . I'm starting to wonder if something terrible happened to him.

Chloe nudges me. "Did you tell him you sleep naked?"

"STOP." I laugh, escaping to the appetizer table. It's full of fresh fruit, finger foods, and bite-sized desserts. The three of us fill our plates, but when we reach the end, Mason turns my direction.

For a second, we just look at each other. Then he lifts his glass in a small, polite salute.

I drop my eyes first. He is handsome, incredibly so, and I don't like that I'm noticing the dimple in his right cheek or the scruff on his jaw.

Jamie might think we need to get out of our comfort zones, but I'm barely finding mine again. I dated Connor for almost two years, knowing deep down the entire time that it wasn't what I wanted. That makes for a rough re-entry into the dating scene. When it's not just the men you don't trust, but yourself.

The night winds down eventually, my friends glowing, tipsy, and thrilled. I make my excuses and head back to the cabin alone. At least Mason doesn't know my friends and can't rat me out for saying I'm tired, only to sit in front of my computer screen until midnight.

Inside, the room is dim, the curtains half drawn. Mason's bag is neatly tucked to one side. Mine sits untouched where I left it.

"Hey." His voice comes from the balcony doorway.

I jump. I hadn't seen him leave the mixer, but then again, I'd very much been not looking. "You need a bell."

He smiles faintly. "Sorry."

We perform the most awkward bedtime choreography known to man. Brushing teeth in shifts, apologizing every time we cross paths. Pretending the other person doesn't exist while being forced to tune in to their every move so we don't accidentally brush arms.

I sit on my bed in shorts and a T-shirt, my bra still on. I don't know how I'm going to survive an entire week like this, but when Mason says, "So. This is fine," I respond with "Totally fine."

I grab my computer from my backpack, and the silence stretches. I want to rip my bra into shreds and light it on fire.

"So. Paramedic, huh?" I start the process of logging in to the WiFi.

He coughs. "Yep."

"Seems stressful." I'm hoping he opts for more than a one-word answer since my curiosity about his life is killing me, but he only says, "Sometimes."

I open my email to find twenty new patient messages and office communications. The people I work with are amazing. Farmers, ranchers, athletes, and new mothers. They're down-home folks with a strong work ethic and grit. Sometimes stubborn as hell, but I'd rather work with that than most other personality issues that lead to noncompliance.

If I were in my own room, I'd turn on one of my playlists, make sure all of my browser windows were open to my most used pages, and dig in. But I'm having a little trouble focusing.

Mason's doing some kind of stretching at the end of his bed. He's wearing joggers and a T-shirt similar to what he'd thrown on in the hall earlier when we visited Guest Services. His clothes all look soft. Like expensive brushed cotton or bamboo or something. The kind of fabric you buy when you value comfort and have opinions about it.

He reaches overhead, fingers lacing together, spine arching. His shirt rides up, and I snap my gaze back to my screen.

"So," he says after a moment, voice casual. "How was the mixer for you?"

I blink. "What?"

"The mixer," he repeats. "Earlier tonight? Not sure how else to say—"

"No, sorry, yeah. That was just way out of context."

His brows pinch. "Out of context? It happened less than an hour ago."

I look up from my screen. "Right. But I was asking you about work." Did this guy have no social or conversational acumen?

He drops onto the bed. "I thought that topic was covered."

I'm not sure what to say to that. If he thinks "yep" and "sometimes" sufficiently explore an area of our lives that consumes at least fifty percent of our time on this planet, then we are very different people.

"The mixer was fine. Didn't look like you were having a blast though," I say.

His eyebrows lift, and I realize that made it sound like I was paying attention to him, which I absolutely was, but don't want to admit.

"I just mean, when I saw you at the bar, you didn't look like you were talking to anyone."

That makes him laugh. A short huff. "Is that bad?"

I shrug. "Depends, I guess. You were at a singles mixer."

He shifts, settling onto his bed, elbows braced on his knees. "Did you meet anyone?"

"Nope." I pop the p.

"Why not?"

"I'm here for my friend's birthday. She's the one who signed us up for the singles stuff. I'm not interested." I don't want to be too critical in case he's actually excited about it.

"Ah." He nods.

I glance up from my screen. "What's that supposed to mean?"

"Nothing." I don't drop my eyes, and he eventually gives. "It's just . . . a little cliché."

My eyes narrow. "Wanting to get work done isn't cliché. We don't all have companies that send us on paid vacations."

His lips twitch. "We don't all have friends who sign us up for 'singles stuff.'" He uses air quotes, then reaches for his bag and pulls out his laptop.

I bite my tongue, debating whether I should say what's on my mind. I wouldn't usually be this bold with someone I just met, but he's the one who opened the door.

I go for it. "So why are you here? Did your work force you to come on singles week?"

His computer chimes as the screen lights up. "Just happened to work out that way."

I study him as he logs in. "So you're not married with kids or something? Just taking advantage of the free drinks?"

He laughs. "No. Definitely not."

"A little cliché," I murmur, turning back to my screen.

"What's a little cliché?" His eyes are on me.

I shrug. "A guy coming on a work trip, pretends he doesn't care, and just happens to be signed up for singles meet-ups."

"That's not at all a cliché."

My head snaps up. "Well, neither is a woman who comes on a cruise with her friend and finds out five minutes before she boards that she's spending seven days meeting guys who want to hook up. Or rooming with one."

He purses his lips. "I don't want to hook up."

"Good."

"And when I said cliché, I was referring to the woman who swears off all dating."

"*So* many women swear off dating. For good reason. That's not a cliché."

"It is when they look like you."

My mouth freezes half open, a flush creeping over my skin. "I—"

"Sorry. I didn't—" He runs a hand through his hair. "I just mean that you're attractive. I'm sure you have plenty of options."

I can't figure out what about that statement pisses me off, so I just start talking. "No, the thing is, nobody has good options right now. Men don't ask women, attractive or not, on dates anymore. They barely talk to us. Even on the apps. And if you do magically happen to meet a guy you're interested in, you have to put forth all the effort and settle for a few texts a week as proof that he might want to get together again at some point. Half the time, they're too wrapped up in sports or gaming or porn to even want intimacy or sex with a real person, and they're definitely too selfish to be good at it anyway, so—"

I suck in a breath, and my cheeks go full tomato when I realize I just spewed all of that in front of a guy I barely know. I give a *there you go* gesture with my hands, then clap them on my thighs. "Sorry. TMI."

I try to shrink over my computer, but Mason does the opposite. He sits straight, his eyes bright. "That's exactly right. Men have too many options to get what they want without giving anything in return. It's safer."

I look up, wary. *Was he agreeing with me?*

The ship sways beneath us. Somewhere down the hall, someone laughs too loudly. A door slams.

Mason exhales. "It sucks. For all of us."

The way he looks furious, like he's ready to incite a revolution to solve this societal mess, makes me laugh out loud.

"What?" He looks like he's not sure if he should laugh with me or not, and that makes his face look even more innocent.

"Are you messing with me?" I don't have enough experience with him to know if he's capable of satire.

"No!" He pushes his laptop to the side and shifts to the edge of the bed. His joggers scrunch at his ankles, and I get a flash of sleepovers from my teenage years. Sitting here with him feels oddly intimate. Not in a sexual way, but in a whispering secrets in the dark kind of way. What I just said? I've never shared that with anyone besides my best girlfriends.

"People are dating less, that's why things like Buoys and Girls week exist, but until we show people how much better real intimacy is, things aren't going to change," Mason says.

I wipe my eyes and push my computer off my lap, turning to him and crossing my legs under me. "But you're not married."

His tongue flicks over his lower lip. "Definitely not."

My stomach flips, and I cross my arms tighter over my middle. "Why? If you're so passionate about real intimacy, why aren't you with someone?"

"I travel a lot."

"So? Women like to travel."

He lets out a puff of air. "It's not fun travel."

I motion to the room. "You're not having fun?"

He grins. "I wouldn't be if I had a woman with me."

That makes me blush again, and we're sitting too close to hide it. I press my palms to my cheeks. "Sorry. I'm tired."

"What are you apologizing for?"

I groan and drop onto my back, pulling the pillow over my face. "Nothing."

Mason laughs and snatches at it, but I hold it tight. "You won't look at me? But we're such good friends already."

"No!" The pillow stifles my laugh. I've always blushed hard, but this whole situation is making me hypersensitive. I'm way out of my comfort zone, and I don't like being vulnerable, and Mason looks insanely hot with his hair all tousled in his loungewear, and he's using big words and agreeing with me. The bar is not very high for my ovaries to start twitching.

"Liv, c'mon." His hand wraps around my wrist, and he tugs.

I finally relent and turn my head, my face on fire. "Fine. Happy?"

His smile stretches wide. "Yes. Thanks." His Adam's apple bobs. "I enjoyed this conversation. And you're cute when you blush."

My breathing stutters, and my lips feel like they're going to combust. He hands me back the pillow, then slides back onto his bed and lifts his computer to his lap. His eyes drop to my mouth for a millisecond before he turns to his screen and clears his throat. "Will the light keep you up if I'm working for a bit?"

I shake my head. "No. I can sleep anywhere."

The corner of his mouth curls. "Not a cliché, then."

Chapter Five

The next day, after a morning run on the track and the breakfast buffet with the girls, we hit the spa. Facials, body wraps, and pedicures take up the majority of our afternoon, so I'm in a good mood fueled by hours with my best friends when we show up to the singles event that night.

The room is laid out like a bad social experiment. Round tables. Two chairs each. A bell at the front. Name tags. A whiteboard that reads: BUOYS & GIRLS WEEK—SPEED DATING.

I stop short in the doorway. "Oh no."

Jamie bumps into my back and immediately squeals, "OH YES."

It's her birthday, I remind myself, as I allow her to drag me in by the hand.

The space buzzes with nervous energy. I'm not going to pretend there aren't attractive men here because there absolutely are. In my early twenties, I would've been thrilled. But now? I'm just tired. Tired of the small talk. Tired of the pretense. My girlfriends are sick of hearing me talk about my dating app idea. I call it Ex-Check, and it's where you connect with an oligarchy of someone's exes and decide whether they're dateable based on *that* information.

"If you ever wonder how much I love you . . ." Chloe trails off, looking like she just swallowed raw fish.

Nina rolls her eyes. "C'mon. This can't be worse than swiping right."

I sigh. "If we only had—"

"Do not say Ex-Check." Tori laughs, and I grin. My job here is done. I don't have to say it for them to all be thinking it anyway.

The five of us move through the room like a school of fish. The staff members hand us name tags and usher us toward the tables.

I spot Mason instantly. He's already seated at one of the tables, elbows resting on the surface, name tag crooked on his chest. He looks relaxed. Observant.

Our eyes meet, and he lifts a brow.

I give a slight shake of my head to make sure he knows the blush rising to my cheeks is from embarrassment and not excitement. *You're cute when you blush.* That line had run through my head for an hour before I finally fell asleep.

What even was that conversation we had? No guy had ever spoken to me like that before.

A staff member encourages us to find our seats, but none of us actually do until the bell rings. After the scramble, I end up across from a guy named Evan, with ocean-blue eyes and a nice smile.

His knee bounces under the table. "So. What's your story?"

"Uh, I'm here for my friend's thirtieth birthday."

He nods. "Where are you from?"

"Montana. I've lived all over, but just moved back a couple of summers ago."

That sets him at ease. His knee still bounces, but at slower intervals. "My parents went to school in Montana."

I reply with the obligatory "That's cool!" and we fall into the typical flow of conversation. Where did you go to school? What do you do for work? It would be easier if we each had a sign around our necks so we could skip answering the same questions over and over.

It's going to be a long night.

Next is Mark, who asks what my astrological sign is and whether I believe in the moon landing. At least that's something new. Then there's Josh, who describes his crypto portfolio in detail without prompting.

Across the room, I catch flashes of my friends. Jamie is laughing, head thrown back, clearly loving something about the guy across from her, who is wearing a Mountain Dew T-shirt and a backward hat.

Tori looks like she's treating this like a police interrogation, and Chloe has her arms and legs crossed, nodding like she's at a job interview.

The bell rings again, and I jolt when my attention slides back to the seat across from me.

"Oh. Hi," I say, and Mason gives a small wave. My mouth is instantly thick.

"Fancy seeing you here." His head cocks to the side, and I can't help but notice that his eyes are greener in this light than in the room.

His foot shifts, and our knees bump together under the table.

"Sorry." He sits up straighter.

I blow out a breath, and am about to say "We don't need to do this," since we're sharing the same cabin, but Mason speaks first.

"What makes you feel most like yourself?"

I blink. *What the hell kind of question was that?* I

scramble for a witty comeback, but the expression on Mason's face makes me pause. He's not smiling. Not teasing me. He looks curious, and after internally complaining about the small talk, I'd be a bit of a hypocrite not to answer thoughtfully.

I glance down at my hands, then back up. My heart races as I say, "I think it's when I'm helping people. I'm a physical therapist, so it's when someone comes in, and I'm able to see what their body needs, then help them through it."

Mason watches me, but doesn't respond. I can't take the silence.

"You know all about that, though," I continue. "Saving lives all day."

He frowns, then nods. "Right."

Again with the one-word answers. Most guys would jump at the opportunity to talk about themselves, to regale me with tales of their heroism on the job or shocking cases.

When Mason is still quiet, I ask the first question that comes to my mind. "What scares you?"

This time, Mason doesn't hesitate. "Wasting time. Doing all the things people tell me to do only to realize later that I missed out."

That was a damn good answer. It hits a little too close to home, so I make a joke. "I would've said choking on a piece of steak in my apartment, but I guess that works."

He smirks. "You like steak?"

"Who doesn't?"

"But you make it at home?"

Now I'm smiling. "Yeah. It's a thousand percent cheaper, and all you have to do is throw it in a cast-iron pan."

"Where do you buy your meat?"

"From a local butcher."

Mason laughs. "I knew it."

"Knew what?"

"You don't seem like someone who'd buy meat at the grocery store."

I drop my mouth in mock horror. "And why is that?"

He motions at me, noting the Lululemon logo on my zip-up.

"Ah. You think I'm rich?" I lean forward, resting my arms on the table. "Joke's on you, then. My parents gave me this jacket for my birthday, and I buy meat at my local butcher because he's a friend of my dad's and gives it to me half off." I give a smug smile. "I'm not rich. I'm practical."

This only makes Mason laugh harder. "I wasn't judging you."

"You were totally judging me."

He grins, opening his mouth to say something, but the bell rings. Mason pauses a moment, then scoots his chair back and stands. Is that . . . a notebook in his back pocket? Who carries an actual notebook these days?

"Good talk." Mason nods once, then moves on to the redhead seated at the table next to mine.

"Hey, I'm Jack." A man in a muscle T with skin the color of my worst blush appears in front of me and throws a hand out to shake. His hand eclipses mine, and if he doesn't have a fever, I'm very concerned about his caffeine intake to achieve this level of vasodilation.

It's more small talk, and I find myself straining to hear what Mason is saying at the other table without turning my head to read his lips. Jack doesn't seem to mind that I'm distracted. Unlike Mason, he's more than happy to talk about himself.

The rest of the hour goes by in a mind-numbing blur, and when Nina suggests the diving show on the top deck, I happily accept.

As we walk to the elevators, I'm still thinking about Mason. Nothing he did or said was what I'd expected, and my mind was fixating on all the discrepancies, as if I were studying an X-ray or an ultrasound.

He had to be gay, right? If he didn't want to hook up, and he communicated so honestly. . . *But was he honest?* He hadn't told me anything about himself, not really.

"Hey, did any of you talk to Mason tonight?" I walk through the sliding glass doors ahead of my friends, and the night air is warm and sticky, even with the breeze over the deck.

"I did," Jamie says, accompanied by nods from Chloe and Tori.

"Not me." Nina makes an "awe shucks" motion with her arm. We walk toward the seating area for the show. A semi-circle of seats, like a mini amphitheatre. Lights ring the diving pool below us, water glowing electric blue.

"Why do you ask?" Chloe gives me a look as we shuffle into the aisle and find an empty block of seats.

"Because he doesn't make any sense." I sit and drop my purse in my lap.

"Did he try something last night?" Nina leans in at the hint of drama.

I laugh and shake my head. "Definitely not." That phrase only makes me think of Mason, which is not helping. "I mean, we talked, but I can't figure him out. What did he say in there with you?"

Tori shrugs. "He likes food. Like, a lot."

My face pinches. "What?"

"He asked what my favorite food was, and when I said sushi, he told me about this great sushi place in Tampa."

My frown deepens. "Okay. So he's from New York, but he knows Tampa sushi places?" He did say he travels a lot.

"He's from New York?" Chloe runs a hand through her hair. "Huh. I would've said West Coast."

"No way," Jamie says. "Midwest for sure. He talked about growing up near the Twin Cities."

I purse my lips. The more I learn about him, the less I know.

"I thought he was a paramedic?" Nina suggests.

I nod. That's what Derek had told me, but had Mason said a thing about his job?

"Maybe his parents moved around. Maybe he's an army brat?" Tori crosses one leg over the other, settling back in her seat.

Chloe chews on her lower lip like she wants to say something. I call her out on it. "No, I was just thinking," she says. "He said something, and now when you reminded me he's a paramedic . . . "

"What did he say?" My heart speeds up.

"I made a joke about that one waiter—the one who had flour or sugar or something on his vest—"

Jamie laughs. "Oh, I saw that guy. He was bringing out the mini cheesecakes."

"Yeah, so I said we should make sure we had the Narcan at the ready." She waits for us to get the joke.

"Because he's obviously doing cocaine. We get it." Tori motions for her to continue, and I snort.

Chloe rolls her eyes. "So, yeah, I made the joke, and he asked what Narcan was."

My eyes narrow. "Was he joking?"

She shrugs. "Would've been *real* dry humor. I don't know. He seemed serious."

Maybe he was kidding about everything. Maybe he was deadpanning, laughing his ass off when we all thought he was serious.

What do I know about Mason? Nothing. Absolutely nothing.

The lights dim, a hush rolling through the crowd as music swells over the speakers.

"Did any of you ask about relationship status? Dating?" I hiss.

Jamie nods. "He hasn't dated anyone in a long time. His words. That's always the first question I ask."

I chew my lower lip. A man in a top hat takes to the stage, but I can't focus. The need to know the truth about my cabin-mate burns through me like Thai food.

What is he hiding? Has anything he's told me been the truth? *And why the hell do I care so much?*

The first diver launches cleanly into the water, and everyone cheers. I clap. I whistle. I laugh at the right moments.

But my brain keeps circling back to Mason sitting across from me. Mason stretching out on the bed. Mason telling me I look cute when I blush.

Eventually, the show ends. People drift off in clumps. I say goodnight to the girls, only half-present in the conversation about Speedos and whether they're attractive or not, then head back to my cabin with Tori since the others decide to hit the tiki bar before turning in.

When I open the door to my room, I stop short.

The beds are pushed together into one queen. With a towel folded into the shape of a heart set on top of the pillows.

Excellent.

I stand there for a full five seconds, brain rebooting. "Cool. Coolcoolcool." I drop my bag, and grab onto the end of the metal bedframe. It won't budge.

I drop to my knees and lift the coverlet to see if the bed's bolted to the floor or something, and when the door opens behind me, I jump.

Slamming my head into the footboard.

Chapter Six

It's a sharp, hollow *thunk* followed by a burst of stars behind my eyes and an immediate, mortifying yelp.

"Son of a—"

"Liv!" Mason rushes toward me. "Hey. Hey. Are you okay?"

"I'm fine." I clutch my head, my skin stinging.

He's already rushing back out the door, and I take the opportunity to check my hand for blood. I press my fingers over the area, and it doesn't feel wet, just hot and swollen.

When he returns a few minutes later, he presses a wrapped towel to the back of my head before I can protest. "Hold this."

I do, swiping at my cheeks. "Where did you find ice?"

"Our room attendant was in the hall. He helped." Mason puts two fingers under my chin and tilts my face up, then stares into my eyes. "Do you feel dizzy?"

I shake my head.

"Nausea?"

"No." I swallow hard. Mason's fingers slowly release, and I try to take a step back, only to have my calves hit the end of the bed.

"What were you doing down there?"

I suck in a breath and motion at the beds. "I was trying to move them back."

Mason nods, then disappears into the hall again. I slump onto the edge of the bed, wincing as blood rushes in my ears. There's a lump forming under the makeshift ice pack, but I tell myself that's a good thing. My mom always said that it was better for swelling to go out rather than in.

The door opens, and Mason reenters the room. "Sorry. I thought I could catch him to fix the beds, but he's not in the hall. I'll just call." He picks up the phone, presses a button, then places the request with someone on the other end of the line.

After hanging up, he hesitates, then scoots past my knees and sits down on the bed next to me. "Sorry I scared you."

"Like I said. You need a bell."

Mason chuckles, rubbing his hands on his thighs. "How was your night?"

"Well, you were there for most of it."

He turns his head. "I was there for the best three minutes, but other than that—"

"Oh, wow. Cocky, are we? Maybe those were my worst three minutes."

"They weren't."

I laugh, and it makes my head throb. Mason must see me wince because his hand flies to my forehead. He presses against it, his other hand covering mine, which is still holding the ice pack.

It's strange having him, or anyone, care for me like this. I'm usually the one holding heat and ice packs on my patients. I'm the one telling them to sit still or asking them to trust me with the movement of their bodies. If he truly is a paramedic, Mason must do this all the time. It's second nature for me when I'm in work mode. Bodies are just bodies, and touching them doesn't mean anything beyond showing a desire to care for another human in pain. But my skin still tingles under his palm.

"Thanks," I whisper.

Mason nods. He doesn't drop his hands. Instead, he guides me back to lie on the bed, turning me to my side so he can keep the ice pack in place. We're nearly spooning when he says, "You didn't like it. The speed dating."

"I hated it," I admit. "It felt like interviewing for a job I didn't want to apply for."

"Why?" His voice is soft.

"Because everyone was trying so hard. That's how those things always are."

"Yeah. I get that. What would have made it better?"

I can't help it. I roll over to face him, losing the ice pack in the process. "Who are you?"

Mason blinks. "I told you, I—"

"No, you didn't tell me. Derek told me. You said you travel for work, but paramedics don't travel, and then you're all . . ."

He studies me. "All what?"

I can't help myself. "Are you gay?"

Mason's eyes widen. Then he lets out a guffaw, rolling to his back and throwing an arm under his head. "No, I'm not gay."

"Okay, I'm sorry! I just—you're a really good listener and—"

"Only gay guys can listen?"

I wince. "So I hear? I don't have a gay best friend, but I've wanted one for ages."

He laughs again, then forces me to lie down, reaching over me for the ice pack and putting it back in place. "I grew up with two sisters."

"You did?"

He nods. "And a single mom. The only people I hung out with growing up were girls."

I look up into his face. He's propped on his elbow, his arm slung over my shoulder, pressing the now-damp towel to my head. His eyes look like the forest in this light.

"You remind me of my oldest sister," he says, and something inside me sinks.

"Oh, yeah?" I try to mask the disappointment, and my voice comes out too bright.

He nods. "She likes to help people, too."

Again. Not at all what I was expecting. It could be the head injury, but for a second, I feel the urge to say something about not wanting him to look at me like a sister.

But then Mason frowns. His face goes gray. Not metaphorically. Actually gray.

"You okay?" I ask.

He swallows hard. "I—" He presses a hand to his stomach.

"Mason?"

"Hold on," he mutters, scrambling back off the bed. He barely makes it to the bathroom before the door slams shut and the lock clicks.

A second later, the sound erupts.

Chapter Seven

Oh, no. Had Mason been motion sick this whole time? Or did he just come down with a stomach bug?

I push up, ignoring the pressure behind my eyes, and stand in front of the door. "Mason?"

Another round of violent misery filters through the door, and it makes my toes curl. "I'm—" he croaks, followed by retching that sounds like it's coming from his soul. "—fine."

I pace the narrow strip of carpet between the beds, my brain ping-ponging between leaving him alone or taking care of him like he just did for me. Towels. Water. Ginger ale. Crackers.

The toilet flushes. The sink turns on. Maybe the shower? My heart twists. Being sick under regular circumstances sucks. Being sick on vacation? The worst.

Mason grunts. "I think the shrimp was bad."

I lean against the door. "You think it's food poisoning?"

"Feels like it."

Did I eat the shrimp? I don't think so. "I'm so sorry."

The door cracks open a few inches, steam spilling out like

he's running a fog machine. I step back. Mason leans against the frame, pale, damp, eyes glassy. "Okay if I shower?"

"Please. Take as much time as you need."

He shuts the door again.

I busy myself with useless tasks. I straighten my suitcase, then set out a bottled water, and am about to look through my snacks to see if I have anything useful when there's a knock at the door.

I open it to find our room attendant, but when I hear the shower turn off, I step out into the hall instead of inviting him in.

"You need the beds moved?" He asks with a smile.

I shake my head. "No, it's fine. He's—Mason's not feeling well. So we'll just deal with it tonight."

"I can—"

"It's okay. If you could move them apart tomorrow?"

He nods. "Of course. Let me know if you need anything else."

I thank him and slip back into the room just as Mason emerges from the bathroom. A towel is wrapped around his waist. His hair is damp, curling at the ends. His skin is flushed, goosebumps raised along his arms. He takes two steps into the room before swaying.

"Careful." I reach out without thinking.

He allows me to steady him, then collapses onto the mattress with a long, shuddering exhale. "I feel like I've been hit by a truck," he mutters.

"I can get you a ginger ale?"

He shakes his head, his cheek pressed to the pillow. "My stomach is still . . . I don't know. I don't think I should eat anything."

I look around for a bucket or a bag. Anything he could use in an emergency. I pull the bag out of the small trash can under the desk. "Here. I'll set this next to your side of the bed."

He gives a half-hearted nod. "Thanks. I'm sorry."

"Stop apologizing. This isn't your fault."

He huffs a weak laugh. His towel is still around his waist, but I don't dare suggest he get up and get dressed. Instead, I pull the comforter out from under him, easy since we'd already messed it up, then drape it over his body. He shivers.

Mason makes a sound. "I'm supposed to be at a meeting tomorrow morning."

I frown. A meeting? Probably virtual. "You could not turn on your camera."

"No, I'm supposed to be up early," he mumbles.

"You might feel better by then. Food poisoning can pass fast." One year at Christmas, my whole family ate bad Chinese food. Every bathroom in the house was in use for twelve hours. We were pale and exhausted, but it led to the best holiday movie marathon I'd ever had.

Mason doesn't answer, so I don't even bother going into the bathroom to change into pajamas. I wash my face and brush my teeth, impressed that there's no proof of Mason's experience besides a pile of his clothes on the floor. Any odor is overpowered by the scent of his body wash.

I take an Ibuprofen for my head, then turn off the lights and crawl into bed. I was planning to do some work, but that's not happening now.

What a ridiculous pair. I have a goose egg on the back of my head, and Mason went from a hundred percent to zero in a matter of seconds.

I pull out my phone and open the Dreamboat app to send a message to the other rooms, and I find a string of messages from my friends. Making plans for getting off the boat in Key West tomorrow morning. Jamie planned a walking itinerary to hit the Hemingway house, Duval Street, and some place that's supposed to have the best Key Lime pie.

They don't want to leave until ten, and it's barely eleven now. Should be plenty of time to get a good rest and be ready to go in the morning.

I plug my phone in and roll over. I'm about to fall asleep when I notice the bed shaking. It's subtle enough, I wonder if it's coming from the ship's engine or something, but then I hear Mason's stilted breathing.

I move a little closer and lift to my elbow.

He's shivering.

I get up and open the bathroom door, flipping on the light to check for extra blankets. There aren't any cabinets, and the closet only has hangers and a shoe rack.

I turn off the light and crawl back onto my side of our joint bed. My hands tingle as I reach out and press my palm to his skin like I'm diffusing a bomb. It's cool and clammy, prickling at my touch.

Damn it. I don't want to make this weird, but he's freezing, and there aren't any extra blankets. Is there even a thermostat?

I consider getting up again to search for it, but my head's pounding, and I just want to close my eyes.

So I do.

I curl up against his side, trying to infuse him with some warmth, and let my head drop into the pillows.

He shifts but doesn't wake. I'm drifting when his breathing evens out. I slip under the second he stops shaking.

* * *

The next thing I know, someone is banging on the door. I jolt awake, disoriented, my cheek pressed to solid warmth.

Mason's chest.

My arm is slung across him, and his arm is tight around me.

The banging continues.

I launch myself out of bed, grateful that my head seems to feel normal, and scramble toward the door, yanking it open—

Derek from Guest Services stands before me. His gaze flicks past my shoulder, and I turn.

Mason lies sprawled across the bed.

Completely naked.

The comforter was pulled off in my quick exit, and his towel is nowhere to be found. The only saving grace is that he rolled over in the few seconds it took me to run to the door .

Derek makes a sound in his throat, and my soul exits my body as I push out into the hall and close the door behind me. "This isn't what it looks like."

"Uh-huh." Derek raises an eyebrow.

"I'm serious, he was—"

"He's late for his meeting, is what he is."

I blink. *How does Derek know about his meeting?*

"He had a rough night." Another eyebrow raise, and I backtrack. "Not like—I mean, he was sick. He didn't sleep well."

Derek shifts on his feet, his face softening. "Well, he's supposed to be at the Buoys Briefing in five minutes."

My pulse kicks up. "The what?"

"The men's meeting. On Modern Dating & Connection. It's part of his contract to observe and provide a write-up."

My grip tightens on the door. The men's meeting? Part of what contract? *Why would a paramedic attend a meeting on dating and connection?*

"I offered to go," I blurt. "To take notes. And he'll do the write-up when he feels better." I think back to the notebook in his back pocket at the mixer. Had he carried one during the speed dating? *Was Mason working for Dreamboat?*

Derek's eyes narrow. "I highly doubt—"

"I won't make a scene, and I'm sure Mason will take care of whatever responsibilities he has. I'll only observe." The idea of sitting in on a meeting where men are talking about dating is almost more intriguing than finding out why Mason is involved.

Almost, but not quite.

Derek agrees, and I rush back into the room. My heart races, my hands start to sweat. I'm going to find out what this men's meeting is all about, and why Mason is supposed to be a part of it.

Chapter Eight

I force my eyes up as I throw the sheets over naked and somehow still sleeping Mason, then quickly change and brush my teeth. It's almost eight in the morning. Plenty of time to do this and come back to grab my things before we get off the ship for the day.

Derek escorts me to a private meeting room on the end of floor six near the swanky Oasis Club where passengers pay to have a private pool and restaurant.

The room is packed with men, and I'm instantly regretting my decision to volunteer for this assignment. What am I doing? Mason might hate me for this. He might hate me for a lot of things, actually. Top of the list? Exposing him to the Dreamboat staff or cuddling up to him while he was asleep. Hopefully he writes it all off as a fever dream.

Ugh. Why did I insert myself into this situation?

I reach for my phone to text the girls, only to realize I left it in my room. *Damn it.* I was so focused on grabbing the notepad and pen on the desk that I didn't think to take it. Now I can't even confess my sins and ask for moral support. Though they'd all probably be sleeping at this hour anyway.

Derek motions for me to make a plate at the small breakfast buffet they have set up with pastries, quiche, and fruit. I do so, then find a chair near the corner and hunker down.

A facilitator, not Derek, steps up to the front. Is he the cruise director? If not, I've definitely seen him on stage around the ship. Maybe he was in the top hat at the diving show?

He waits for the room to quiet, and I scan for people I recognize. Many of the guys taking their seats have been at the mixer and speed-dating events. I spot the guy Jamie was laughing with and Jack, the guy who stopped at my table after Mason last night.

Many of them glance my direction, a little wary. If anyone should be nervous, it's me. I've never been in a room alone with this many men, ever.

"Welcome to the Buoys Briefing: Modern Dating & Connection," the facilitator says. "My name is Garrett, nice to meet you, and we're going to go through a series of statements. I'd like to get your take on them. This is a discussion, not a lecture." He flips to the first card in his hand and reads, "Connection is not performance," then looks out at the participants. "Thoughts?"

The room is dead silent.

Garrett lets it stretch, unbothered. He's wearing dark slacks and a fitted polo with the Dreamboat logo, headset mic looped over one ear.

Finally, a guy in the second row clears his throat.

"I mean." He rubs the back of his neck, "That sounds nice, but . . ."

A few heads nod, and a couple of guys chuckle.

A man near the aisle—built, mid-thirties, wearing a backward cap—shrugs. "Women say they don't want specific things, but, you know. They actually do. We have to make a good impression, and we have to be good at . . . stuff."

More laughs.

Garrett grins. "Okay, perfect. So what does 'making a good impression' usually look like?"

"Talk yourself up," someone mutters.

"Be funny," another says.

"Nah, ask questions about her."

Garrett nods. "Okay, okay. Let me ask you this: How many of you have been on dates where you felt like you were auditioning?"

Every single hand goes up.

Garrett continues, "Right. Now, how many of you have been on a date where it felt like the other person was auditioning?"

Again, hands.

"Does it feel that way whenever you meet someone new? Or just women?" Garrett asks.

The men's hands lower, their expressions shifting to everything from pensive to confused.

"That's why I don't like to meet new people," a man with a shaved head and gauges in his ears says. A few other guys nod in agreement.

I think back to my conversation with Mason. Talking about men being scared is one thing, but seeing it right in front of me? Instead of being pissed about the dating scene, I'm starting to second-guess my self-righteousness. What was it Mason said? *It sucks for all of us.* Were men *and* women the victims here?

Garrett blows out a breath. "Good. Food for thought. Here's our next statement: Curiosity beats confidence."

This one gets an immediate reaction.

"No way," someone blurts.

"Confidence is all women want," another guy chimes in.

Jack says, "I asked a lot of questions last night. Didn't help."

"What kind of questions?" Garrett asks.

Jack hesitates. "Like . . . what do you do. Where are you from. What are you looking for."

I think back to my three minutes with him. He had asked a few questions, but mostly he'd talked about himself.

Garrett nods. "And were you actually interested in the answers?"

Jack frowns. "I mean, yeah?" He pauses for a beat. "Mostly?"

There's a ripple of laughter.

"Here's what the data shows." Garrett pulls out another card. "When women report feeling chemistry, it's less about how impressive someone was and more about whether they felt seen."

Several guys shift in their seats.

"Seen how?" someone asks.

"Like the person across from them was actually present," Garrett explains. "Listening. Responding. Letting the conversation go somewhere unexpected."

I stare down at my notepad. Crap. I hadn't written down a single thing. I start scribbling down the highlights, but my mind is circling that last statement from Garrett. That's precisely what Mason did, and while I wasn't going to say anything, I could verify that it did indeed have an effect on me.

A guy near the wall crosses his arms. "That sounds exhausting."

"It can be. If you're trying to control the outcome. Connection isn't about getting a result. It's about honest interest in another human being." Garrett lets that sink in, then flips to another card. "Statement three: If she says she's not looking for a relationship, believe her."

"Women never say they're looking for a relationship," someone says immediately. "They're supposed to be all independent now. Say they don't need us."

"That's a trap." Another guy laughs. "Women say that all the time, and then they end up getting with someone else."

Garrett smiles. "But you're interested, so what do you do?"

Jack catches on first. "Curiosity. Real connection. No expectations."

"Gold star, my friend!" Garrett pretends to pull out a sticker and press it to Jack's chest.

I keep writing, not sure I'm getting everything down correctly, especially with my head spinning like this. I'm impressed. Shocked. And oddly hopeful. These types of comments, and their willingness to be open, are the most attractive things I've witnessed in years.

What is Mason's involvement in this? I thought coming to the meeting would answer my questions, but instead, it's only multiplied them.

"But what if she never gets interested?" One man asks, the one Jamie was laughing with on night one.

Garrett draws a breath. "Yeah. It'll happen for sure. Putting yourself out there, trying to connect, it's risky. But d'you know what's also risky?" He pulls out another card. "Here's what the data tells us. Men who experience prolonged loneliness, especially men who stop trying to form real, vulnerable connections, are significantly more likely to struggle with depression, anxiety, substance use, and suicidal ideation."

The room stills.

Garrett goes on. "And here's the part most people get wrong. The biggest risk factor isn't rejection. Rejection hurts. It stings. It bruises the ego. But it's finite." He taps the card against his palm. "Isolation is not."

Garrett looks up. "What we see over and over is men deciding that staying home is safer. That not asking is better than hearing no. That avoiding the situation altogether protects them." He pauses. "It doesn't."

Holy hell. This was not what I was expecting at eight in the morning. My nose starts to sting. *Am I going to cry right now?* I sniff and finish writing a summary of what Garrett just said.

A guy in the back lifts his hand halfway. "So we're just supposed to keep putting ourselves out there?"

Garrett nods. "Yes. Connection isn't a guarantee. But avoidance guarantees disconnection."

Another guy speaks up, quieter. "It's exhausting. To keep trying."

I swallow hard. This isn't theoretical, and it's not just reality for the men in this room. My sadness turns to a silent rage. How did this happen? How did we, as humans, grow so far apart in our communication, cultural opportunities, and gender roles, that nobody is getting the relationships they want?

Derek taps my shoulder, and I jump. He nods toward the door. It takes me a second, but when I remember I don't have a purse or a phone, I press my pen to the notepad and stand from my chair to follow.

* * *

I stop at Jamie and Chloe's cabin first and get no answer, then try Tori and Nina. Nothing. They probably messaged me about hitting the breakfast buffet, but since I left my phone in the room, I had no idea.

I scan my wristband and enter my room to find Mason upright. Showered, dressed, hair still damp.

I try to smile like a normal person. "You look better."

He eyes me. "Where were you?"

"Uhhh . . ."

Mason's eyes drop to the notepad in my hand.

My cheeks flush. "I went to a meeting."

"My meeting?"

My face falls. "I'm sorry. I didn't know what to do. Derek—"

"No, Liv. Stop." He holds up a hand. "I'm not interrogating you."

I purse my lips. "Are you mad?"

He shakes his head. "Did you get some good notes?"

"I think so." I swallow hard, shifting on my feet. I had to ask him. "What do you do, Mason?"

His brow twitches. "Derek didn't tell you?"

I shake my head. "He said you had to be at the meeting, and I can't quite figure out why a paramedic would be needed at a meeting about connection—"

"Yeah. Derek has a sense of humor."

My heart speeds. Not out of fear, but anticipation. And then out of panic because I catch the time on the clock in my peripheral vision.

I curse under my breath and bolt for my swimsuit. As much as I'm dying to hear the rest of the story, it's already nine thirty-five. "My friends are probably waiting for me. I—"

There's a knock at the door. I turn to Mason, my eyes pleading. He gets up and walks to the door while I pop into the bathroom to change. I yank off my shirt and bra.

"Uh, Liv?" Mason raps his knuckles on the bathroom door.

I freeze. "Yeah?"

"You should come out here."

"I'm not dressed."

There are murmured voices, then Mason says, "Just throw something on. They need to talk to us both."

They? I fight with my swimsuit top, finally get it on, then yank open the door to find Mason standing at the door with a petite staff member in a white coat. She's also wearing a mask.

She smiles politely. "Good morning. We just need to inform you both of a temporary health precaution. Because

Mr. Reyes experienced gastrointestinal symptoms last night, we're required to perform an oral swab and place the cabin in quarantine until we see a negative test result—"

"A what?"

She repeats herself and holds up two plastic vials. "A negative test result."

"No, I understand that part, but you said quarantine?"

"Correct. Out of an abundance of caution."

Mason leans against the wall. "I'm positive it was food poisoning."

The woman nods. "Right. As soon as we can confirm there are no positive test results—"

"How long will that take?" I ask.

"Typically less than twenty-four hours."

"Twenty-four hours?" I don't mean to sound rude, but the plans for my entire day with friends are crashing around me. "But I'm supposed to get off the boat. And I haven't had any symptoms."

"I understand, Miss, but you'll need to remain in your cabin until we can confirm." She gives me a pitying smile. "Room service will be provided."

I look at Mason. His expression is grim as he mouths, "I'm so sorry."

The staff member looks between the two of us, holding out the vials. "If you'll allow me to swab your cheeks?"

I groan and stalk back into the room to grab my phone. I need to send some messages.

Chapter Nine

LIV:

Sorry I missed these. Crazy morning. SO
MUCH TO TELL YOU

But I won't be joining you in Key West

QUARANTINED

JAMIE:

WHAT!? Why!?

TORI:

Are you sick???

NINA:

With Mason? • •

LIV:

Not sick, but Mason got food poisoning. I
mentioned it to a staff member, and I think
they must've reported it? We had to do
cheek swabs

JAMIE:

NOOOOOOOOO. Are you serious?

CHLOE:

Is Mason okay?

LIV:

Fine. Oh. And I saw him naked

TORI:

Ummm lead with that please

NINA:

Like saw him naked or saw him naked? 😅

LIV:

He threw up in the bathroom and barely
made it to the bed wrapped in a towel.

So.

Saw him naked

JAMIE:

LOL!!!

CHLOE:

You can't make this shit up

TORI:

How long is the quarantine?

. . .

Liv:

> Until we get test results. Maybe I can still
> get out of here? Meet you on the island?

Jamie:

> I've got great service. Just text and we'll
> meet you wherever! So sorry, babe…

* * *

I drag my hands down my face, sprawled on the bed, still wearing my bikini top with my unbuttoned jeans. "This is ridiculous."

Mason sits on the chair, a plate of plain toast sitting beside a cup of ginger beer. They didn't have ginger ale, so this was the closest they could get. "I'm sorry. I—"

"No, it's not your fault."

"Kind of is."

I blow out a breath and roll onto my stomach. "It's their fault for poisoning you."

Mason opens the blinds, and we have a perfect view of the shore from our windows. It's a gorgeous sunny day with palm trees waving lazily in the sea breeze. "I'm supposed to be walking along that beach right now."

"Maybe the swab will come back quickly."

I nod. This is probably the best port to be in, given the unpredictable schedule. Everything's walkable. "I was really looking forward to the Hemingway house."

Mason turns to look at me. "Why?"

I squint at him like he just asked why water is wet. "Because he was crazy."

Mason laughs. "Obviously."

"No, I'm serious." I plunk my chin in my hands. "He was crazy, but he didn't try to shut it down like the rest of us." Mason watches me, and it makes me nervous, so I keep talking. "Like, is that what it takes to do something extraordinary? Lean into our vices, stop trying to fit the mold, and make a mess of most of our relationships?"

"Sounds like a question for Hemingway house." Mason drops onto the bed next to me.

"Exactly. That and whether I need a six-toed cat."

He scoffs. "That's a no-brainer." From this angle, with the sun pouring through the window, it looks like one side of his face has been dipped in gold. "What?" He catches me staring.

I clear my throat and look away. "You didn't finish your thought. Earlier." I feel his eyes on me, on my exposed stomach. I want to suck in and make it look flatter, but don't want to be obvious that I noticed, so I resist the urge.

"Which one?" His voice lowers with the question, and it quickens my pulse.

"About Derek. About you going to meetings."

Mason nods, blowing out a breath. "I should've explained the first night. I honestly . . . I didn't think we'd be talking much."

I turn to meet his eyes. "What does that mean?"

He gives a sheepish smile. "I don't know. You seemed pretty pissed about the whole room situation."

"I was pissed. You didn't seem so happy yourself."

"Exactly. Neither of us wanted to be here. We both had work, so I figured it didn't matter what you thought I was."

I take a note out of his book and stay quiet, waiting for him to expound on that thought. It works.

"Derek thought it would be funny if I had a back story."

Mason rubs the back of his neck. "I worked on this ship six months ago to help them start the Buoys and Girls program. The research on connections and relationships is brutal. People are lonelier than they've ever been, even with the rise of 'happy and single' narratives."

I frown. "I'm happy and single."

"So if you met the right guy, you'd choose single over being with him?"

I open my mouth, then close it. "Well, no, but I don't think there is a right guy."

Mason's mouth curls up. "Exactly. If you can't get what you want, convince yourself to want what you can get."

I push myself higher on the bed and curl into the pillows so I can look at him without craning my neck. "So you're saying I'm lying to myself."

"No. You're making the best of it. It's admirable."

"That sounds super patronizing."

Mason laughs. "Sorry. If it makes you feel better, you're not alone. Dreamboat realized that singles cruises were selling out faster than anything else in the industry. Not because people wanted hookups, contrary to popular belief, but because they wanted permission to meet people in person without it being weird."

"People are sick of dating apps."

"Yeah. So they brought me in to figure out why their traditional singles events weren't yielding connections. Lots of flirting and conversation. Lots of numbers exchanged. Almost zero follow-up."

"Because it's all surface level."

"Bingo," he says. "So I helped them redesign the experience. You can still do the typical fun dating stuff, but people need to have an intention."

I consider this. "So you're teaching them. That's what the meeting was."

Mason slides fully onto the bed, leaning against the headboard next to me. "That's the goal. It's all experimental."

"So are you a therapist or something?"

He nods. "I am."

My ribs tighten. What have I said to him over the past two days? Has he been analyzing me this whole time? Judging my responses?

"But nobody really knows what they're doing in this realm, including me," Mason says.

I raise an eyebrow. "Uh, it seems like you know what you're doing."

He turns to look at me. "Don't love your tone on that sentence."

I laugh. "Well? This is your job. So you know what to say and not say. It's all scripted, right?"

Mason's smile fades. "Scripted? Which part?"

"Like your conversations with women. You know what to say—"

"Liv, I'm still human. Yes, I've learned good communication skills that are helpful when talking with anyone, but that doesn't mean—"

"No, yeah. I get it." I roll to my back, trying to figure out why my throat is so thick. "So why did you go along with Derek's cover story?"

Mason exhales. "I wanted to experience the program the way a guest would. See what worked. What didn't. What people actually talked about when they thought no one important was listening. But I was supposed to have my own room so I could decompress."

I nod, now staring straight ahead at our closed cabin door. "Right. That can be draining." My chest feels like a shaken Coke, so I push myself to the end of the bed and stand. "I'm going to change. Get some work done—"

"You seem mad," Mason cuts in.

"Mad?" I scoff. "I'm not mad. Just adjusting to a new plan for the day."

"I didn't mean to lie to you, but I realize that's what I did. I'm sorry."

My breathing quickens. What am I supposed to say to that? What I want is for him to say something I can push against. Something that would make me feel even a little bit justified in how I feel right now, but instead, he just apologizes?

I plant a hand on my hip. "That wouldn't work on me."

Mason frowns. "What wouldn't?"

"All of the relationships stuff they taught in the meeting. Even if you make a connection, there's always something. Something you don't know—"

"Well, of course there is. You're two totally different people. Hopefully, you'll be discovering new things about each other forever."

"Hopefully?" I scoff. "People hide the things they're not proud of. It's not fun to 'discover.'"

"So you want to know everything about someone before you get together."

I nod. "Yep."

"So you don't want that person to keep learning and growing? To change and become better over time?"

"No, that's not what I'm saying."

Mason nods. "Maybe not. But it sounds to me like you're saying you don't believe someone can have character. That they can show up consistently over time."

"That's exactly what I'm saying. People can seem one way on vacation or in a bar or a friend's house, and then be someone totally different at home. You can't really know a person, so why would I ever take that risk?"

He draws a breath and lets it out slowly. "I think you only need to know the most important things."

I tap my foot on the carpet. "Maybe. But it would take a lot of proof to make me want to date again." He might be right that choosing to be single was a cop-out, but I understood the guys from this morning's meeting. Why keep putting yourself out there when all it's brought you is pain? And if I have good friends? Good connection? Then I'm not exactly at massive risk of isolation or loneliness.

"And what could someone do to prove it to you?" Mason asks. Another question I don't have a response to. "Or, maybe a better question is, what would you do to prove yourself to them?"

Chapter Ten

That wasn't a better question. It was a stupid question. One that I think about for longer than necessary as I stand under the shower stream, letting the water pound against my shoulders.

I scrub shampoo into my hair and tilt my head back, eyes closed. It's unsettling how much sense he makes. I've spent the last six months telling myself I'm better off. Happy. Which is true. Mostly. But maybe I've also been strategic. Avoiding situations where I might put myself at risk of wanting.

You know, like sharing a cruise cabin with a hot therapist.

I rinse, and when I step out, I skip anything remotely cute and pull on soft joggers and a tank top. I don't make the decision not to put a bra on, but when I walk out, I realize I forgot. I throw on a long-sleeve cotton shirt, then join Mason on the balcony. The ocean stretches out beyond him, sun flashing off the water.

"No word yet?" I ask. He shakes his head. We order room service. Sandwiches, fries, and Caesar salad to make ourselves feel good about our choices, then settle into a quiet rhythm of scrolling and typing.

I answer emails. He types something, glancing at the notes I gave him from the meeting that morning. The breeze lifts the edge of his papers, and I reach over without looking to pin them down with my hand.

At one point, I laugh out loud at the words on my screen.

"What?" Mason asks.

"I have a patient who just emailed me to ask if coffee counts as water."

He squints. "Well?"

I laugh. He doesn't need me to answer that for him.

Mason smiles, genuine and warm. "You love your patients."

"I do. Even when they're high-maintenance."

"Especially when they're high-maintenance?"

A blush lifts to my cheeks. "Maybe."

Mason sets his laptop on the table between us. "Tell me about your friends."

I raise an eyebrow. "Why?"

"Because I'm curious."

I think about calling him out, telling him he's using his techniques on me, but it feels nice that he's asking. So I tell him about Jamie. How she's fearless but cries in good commercials. About Chloe's dry humor, critical eye, and huge heart. About Nina's free spirit and Tori's practicality. He listens like he's filing away each detail. He doesn't look at his phone once.

"You're all lucky," he says. "Good friends who put forth effort are hard to come by."

I nod. "So what about you?"

He runs his hand over his jaw. "My brother's my best friend. And I talk with a few close friends from my master's program."

"They're therapists, too?"

"Yep."

"Do you share crazy stories?"

He grimaces. "I can't share client details."

"Oh, please. Are you that strict? No names, no identifying info. It's totally fine."

He gives me a look that says, "Not really," but I press him.

"How are you supposed to carry all of that on your own? Without *connection* to process it?"

Mason laughs. "Okay."

"I'm serious." I like that he finds me funny. I like talking to him, and that my comments seem to surprise him just as much as his throw me off guard. "Tell me one."

"No."

"C'mon. There's no way I'll ever meet these people."

"I mean, you might."

I wave him off. "I live in rural Montana."

He hesitates, then exhales. "Okay. One."

I sit back, delighted. "Yes."

"There was this consultation," he begins. "Supposed to be for a mid-sized company. Retention issues. Low morale. Standard stuff."

"Uh-huh." I lean forward, resting my face in my hands.

Mason's mouth quirks, and he seems to lose his train of thought for a moment. "I show up, and there was only one woman. No team. No HR rep. Just her."

"At a house?"

He shakes his head. "No. An office in Jersey." He clears his throat. "She proceeds to spend forty-five minutes explaining how she's running an experiment, and because she wasn't sure if my methods were proven, she wanted to start small and then scale."

I cover my mouth. "Oh no."

"She asked if just the two of us could meet—"

"Oh, you're so innocent."

He groans. "When she started unbuttoning her blouse—"

I burst out laughing. "Stop!"

"She offered to double my fee."

"Did you say yes?"

"Liv." He gives me a look. "I declined. Respectfully."

I lean back in the deck chair. "See? You can't keep stories like that inside your body."

Mason makes a sound in his throat and turns to look out at the water, then starts to reach for his laptop.

"Do you want to watch a movie?" I ask. My emails are all answered, and I haven't watched a movie with someone in months. Mason doesn't give an immediate yes, so I backtrack. "Or I can just watch by myself if you have more work—"

"No, I was just going to say we should put these dishes out." He motions to the remnants of our lunch.

I help him move the plates and cups to the hall. When I set them down, he moves them closer to our door.

"Very precise," I murmur.

He frowns. "Just trying to be considerate."

I straighten and look up at him. "You don't like that."

"What?"

"Being told you're uptight." Both times I'd teased him about that today, he tensed.

Mason blinks. "Huh." We walk back into the room, and he holds the door for me. "When I was a kid, my older brother was the fun one. He was always getting us into trouble."

"You didn't like that?"

Mason runs a hand through his hair. "No. I loved and hated it. I wanted to jump into his crazy plans, but I was always too scared."

I crawl onto the bed and slide under the covers.

"Maybe I still want to be more like him." He picks up the remote control and settles on the bed next to me.

"Or maybe that's why you still have him in your life," I say.

He pauses with the remote pointed at the TV. After a second, he clicks and navigates to the movie channel. *When Harry Met Sally* is one of the first that pops up, and when Mason says he's never seen it, I insist that he press play.

We half-watch it, half-talk over it, arguing over whether straightforward communication is always best because sometimes mystery and subtlety is a good thing. We talk about friendships, attraction, and of course, frequency of faked orgasms, and when the movie ends, I realize I haven't thought once about getting our swabs back.

We order more food, including chocolate-dipped strawberries and champagne, because if Mason's going to throw up again, it might as well be bubbly.

By nine o'clock, we decide we may as well go to bed since it doesn't seem like we're getting turn-down service. Makes sense, considering.

When the lights are out, I lie on my back, staring into the pitch black.

"Hey, Liv?" Mason's voice lifts to my right.

"Hm?"

"There's something we need to talk about."

I roll to my side. "Okay."

He shifts, and I wonder if he's facing me. "You saw me naked."

I nearly choke on my spit. "I—I was at the door, and I promise, I didn't look. Like, I saw, but I didn't—"

Mason's laugh rises, cutting me off. "You saw, but you didn't what?"

My face is red hot, and I'm glad he can't witness it this time. "I didn't stare! I tried to just cover you up."

"Tried?"

"No, I did!" I groan and throw an arm over my face. "I did my best, okay? You were passed out, and your towel disappeared."

"I found it actually."

"You did? Where was it?"

"Your side of the bed."

That shuts me up.

Mason clears his throat. "I was cold. Last night. I think I was shivering."

"Yeah. You were. I—"

"Thank you. You didn't need to do that."

Blood rushed in my ears, and I work to swallow. "You're welcome. I like taking care of people."

There's another shift in the sheets. "I do, too."

We lie there in silence for a moment.

"Do you want a massage?" Mason asks, and I think my heart stalls for two beats.

"Uh . . ."

"Not like—you know, like an actual massage. I just feel bad you had to sit in this room all day, and I wanted to do something for you."

I can't think. Somewhere, practical thoughts are probably trying to break through the haze of imagining Mason's hands on my skin, but they aren't successful.

Instead, I hear myself say, "Okay. That would be nice."

Chapter Eleven

Mason's hands are on my skin.

I'm lying on my stomach in my tank top, my bottom half still covered by the sheets. Mason sits next to me like this is entirely normal. Like he gives apology massages to random female roommates regularly.

He inhales, and the sound reverberates through my spine. "Sorry. Are my hands cold?"

I shake my head, then realize he can't see it since we didn't turn on any lights. Stupid move. Lying here in the dark makes me hypersensitive to every sound and every movement he makes, and my brain makes every single one lean erotic. It's been way too long since a man has touched me like this for me to expect anything less. The massage from the Hungarian grandma in the spa definitely didn't count.

Mason's thumbs press into the base of my neck. The pressure is firm. Slow.

A noise escapes me that I pray is mostly muffled by the pillow.

Mason's hands pause. "Too much?"

"No," I croak. "That was . . . it's perfect."

He makes a soft sound that might be a laugh. Then he continues, slow and steady, working down the muscles along my shoulders.

I close my eyes and will myself not to imagine him shirt-less. *He is wearing a shirt, isn't he?*

This is the problem with Mason. He's so damn calm. So sure of himself. I'm like a cat who can sense he'll never force-hold me or rub my belly unless I ask him to, and it's sexy as hell. Also, I kind of want him to force-hold me.

What is wrong with women? We want guys to be assholes, but only when we want them to be assholes. They're supposed to be nice, then take control, embody sensitivity, and also be mysterious and hard to get.

Sure, there are a thousand unrealistic expectations for women, too, but I'm beginning to think we are a part of the problem.

"Your shoulders are so tight," he murmurs.

"Mmhmm," I manage, because my ability to form sentences is also currently in quarantine.

His fingers dig into a knot near my shoulder blade, and I swear I see my life flash before my eyes. Mostly the late nights charting patient notes while clenching my jaw hard enough to crack enamel.

"You ever think you work too much?" he asks.

I sigh. "Maybe." But what else would I do? I must say that last part out loud because he huffs a laugh.

"I understand that."

Mason's hands slide lower, thumbs pressing along the ridge of muscle beside my spine. Heat blooms across my back, spreading outward like a slow wave. My skin tingles. My thoughts go fuzzy.

When he's finished there, he shifts, bracing one hand on my shoulder while the other works into the muscle at the base of my neck again. My entire body melts into the mattress.

He moves to my arms, kneading along my triceps, and I audibly sigh. This time, Mason doesn't comment.

How in the hell am I going to explain this to my friends? Because when I walk out of that room in the morning, I am not going to be the same person, and they're all going to see it.

Oh, you know, just a casual massage in the dark with my assigned roommate after holding him naked all night. A typical Tuesday.

By the time Mason's hands stop, I feel loose and floaty. He draws back and clears his throat. "Okay."

I blink, disoriented.

He pulls my tank top back down, and the bed dips as he moves back to his side. "Goodnight, Liv."

Hm. Yes. Goodnight. Tell that to the circulation you just activated, all of it seeming to pool in one central location.

"Hm?" he asks, and I cough.

"Oh, nothing. Goodnight. And thank you."

At first, I think I'm going to lie awake all night, but my thoughts fade within minutes. When I drift to sleep, it's deep and heavy. The kind I haven't had in months.

* * *

I wake to Mason's alarm, though my phone buzzes on the nightstand seconds after I blink my eyes open. The blinds are good enough that it's still solidly black in our room, and Mason slides out of bed to let in some light.

I sit up, hair wild, blinking. "What time is it?"

Mason unplugs his phone. "Seven. Sorry to wake you."

I yawn. "Only nine hours of sleep. Pathetic."

He chuckles. "Mind if I shower?"

I wave him toward the bathroom. As soon as he's finished, I get in, hoping I'll regret wasting the time because I'll be diving into the ocean with my friends in an hour.

Last night—the whole day really—feels like a time warp. Those twenty-four hours seemed to stretch until I didn't remember my life before I was stuck in this cabin with Mason.

My skin tingles when I remember talking with him in the dark. His hands on my skin.

I shiver and turn off the water, then wrap myself in a towel and realize my clothes are back in the room.

Well. If Mason can do it, so can I.

I hike the towel up only to have it hit dangerously high on my thigh. Which is worse? I determine cleavage is more appropriate than full frontal, and step out into the room.

"Hey, sorry I—" I stop dead. The cabin is clean. Not "just made the bed" clean, but professionally. The little clutter we'd amassed is gone. The sheets are crisp. The room smells of citrus.

I turn to see our room attendant, and he drops his eyes. "Sorry, Miss. I was going to do the bathroom—"

"No, please." I open the door for him and shuffle further into the room.

Mason stands at the door to the balcony, arranging something on the table. I forget I'm only wearing a towel and step up to the threshold.

"What is this?"

He jolts and straightens. "You need a bell."

I grin, noting the muscle that twitches in his jaw as his eyes flick down a couple of inches, then snap back up.

He clears his throat. "This is a celebration."

"For?" There's a full breakfast spread. A real one. Not sad room-service cereal. There's a tray with fruit, pastries, eggs, toast, little jars of jam, and a pot of coffee. Two plates set. Two mugs.

"Our freedom."

I gasp. "Shut up."

Mason laughs. "Our swabs came back negative, and since

we have no other symptoms, we are free to move about the ship."

The news settles into me in layers. It's good news. I've been dying to get together with the girls, and even more desperate to get out on the beach, but there's also a twinge of something beneath my ribs.

"Well. That's great to hear."

He nods once. "It is."

My toes curl against the industrial carpet. "I'll get dressed." I spin and take the four steps to the end of the bed to find my clothes. Our room attendant is just finishing up with our bathroom, so I take a moment to text Jamie and let her know I'll be there for the excursion. We have to meet on the dock at 8:30, which should give me plenty of time to eat.

When our room attendant leaves, I thank him and step into the bathroom to change. My stomach growls, and I move faster, putting on my bikini and cover-up dress. There's no way Mason put all that together while I was in the shower. Which meant he probably arranged the delivery at some point last night. How had he done that without me noticing?

I hurry back out and sit. We dish up and eat in comfortable quiet for a few minutes, then the conversation starts up like it always does with Mason. A question.

"So." He tears off a piece of croissant. "Tell me about your ex."

I nearly choke on a sip of coffee. "Excuse me?"

"You must have one."

I scoff. "What if I didn't? That question would be very offensive."

"I'll take my chances." He smirks, and I exhale.

"He was fine. At first. Then it became clear he wanted the benefits of a relationship without any of the responsibility, and I let it happen."

"Why?"

I shrug. "Because I liked the idea of him."

"Good looking?"

"Hockey player."

Mason chortles. "They're having a moment."

"Definitely." I take two pieces of pineapple. "Okay. Your turn."

He takes a sip of orange juice. "She was brilliant. Laughed at all my jokes."

"That sentence doesn't corroborate the first."

He winks at me. "It's okay if you're jealous."

I snort. "Was she a doctor?"

"She was. Brain surgeon."

My smile fades. "You're serious?"

"As a neuroblastoma."

I roll my eyes. "Welp. There goes my plans for the day."

"What plans?"

"I was going to set you up with Tori, but she's only a pediatrician."

"Hm. Definitely not up to par."

We talk about families, mine in Montana and Idaho, his parents in Florida and his brother in New York. He tells me his mother still tries to set him up with "nice girls" from church. I tell him my dad thinks any man who doesn't know how to skin an elk won't be able to protect me in the apocalypse. Mason agrees they probably couldn't.

I eat the last of my fruit slower than necessary, then take a final sip of my lukewarm coffee. "Well. This was lovely. Thank you."

"You're welcome. I think we made the best of this situation." His hair falls over his brow, and he smooths it back. There's scruff on his jaw, and I fight the urge to reach over and run my fingernails over it.

"Very admirable," I say, repeating his words from day one.

Mason's eyes lock on mine, then he sets his glass on the table. "Have a good day with your friends."

"You too. I mean, with your meetings."

He laughs. "You'll definitely win this round."

I tap the edge of my glass. "Okay."

Mason watches me, the corner of his mouth still lifted. "Okay."

Chapter Twelve

The ocean is still waking up when we meet on the pier. It's that early-morning kind of blue. Sleepy, glassy, like it hasn't decided yet whether it's going to be friendly or raucous. The sun is already blazing, and the air smells like salt and brine.

Jamie bounces on the balls of her feet like she needs to pee. She's in a bright coral swimsuit, a white cover-up, and a bucket hat that makes her look like a SoCal hot mom.

Tori is in practical black, hair swept back, carrying a small dry bag, which I'm definitely planning to share. Chloe wears sunglasses and a baseball cap, and Nina wears a patterned vintage swimsuit with tiny lemons and an oversized straw tote.

Jamie claps her hands together. "Is everyone manifesting turtles?"

We nod like her obedient children, then fall into step with the line of other cruisers, and a cluster of guys falls in behind us. At the sound of their voices, far too chipper for eight-thirty in the morning, I realize they're the guys we saw at boarding and briefly encountered during the singles events.

One of them wears a muscle shirt, pretty sure I remember

him from the meeting. Another has sunglasses perched on his head like he's about to sell me a timeshare.

"Ladies. We on the same boat?" Muscle Shirt Guy raises an eyebrow.

Chloe mutters, "If one of them says 'low-key' or 'lit,' I'm swimming back to Miami."

"Hey, Ben." Jamie waves, and Muscle Shirt Guy gives her a head nod.

"You know him?" Tori hisses.

Jamie nods. "We speed dated. Didn't you?"

The rest of us shake our heads. There had to be over a hundred people at those events. We would've had to stay there for hours to meet them all.

The ocean wakes up for the boat ride. The water is choppy enough to bounce my stomach around, and the guide is trying to explain safety rules with a Mexican accent over a speaker that keeps breaking up. Thankfully, I've gone snorkeling before and know the basics.

"You okay?" Tori asks over the rush of the wind.

"Yeah!" I call back.

"You look a little melancholy."

I shake my head and give her a squeeze. Was I thinking about Mason? Wondering what he was doing at that moment? Wondering if he was thinking about me?

Possibly. But I quickly recalibrate. I came on this cruise for girl time. Sunshine. Friendship. Laughing until my cheeks hurt. I did not come to obsess over some guy.

I tip my head toward her and say, "I'm good!"

Tori nods just as Ben, Muscle Shirt Guy, leans in from the opposite bench. "I didn't get your names!"

Tori and I introduce ourselves, and he introduces his friends, Luke, Kipp, and Jake. They're from the Portland area.

"You all here for Buoys and Girls Week?" Ben asks.

"We're here for our friend's birthday trip." I point to Jamie.

"Nice," he says. "But you're doing the singles stuff too, right?"

I glance at Jamie, who's currently chatting with one of the other guys like they're old pals, and then at Chloe, who looks like she's considering throwing herself overboard out of pure spite.

"Yes," Tori says, shooting me a look. "Some more willingly than others."

Ben laughs like that's adorable. "That's when you find love. When you're not looking for it."

Tori groans. "So cliché."

The word sends bubbles through my center, and I hold back a smile. I'm dying to debrief the girls. Here on the boat is not the time, considering I can barely understand simple sentences over the roar of the engine, but maybe we can circle up on the beach before lunch.

The guide announces we're nearing the reef, and everyone starts gearing up. We adjust our masks and hold onto the fins he passes out. Someone drops a snorkel and curses, and our guide then teaches the whole boat how to swear in Spanish.

The moment we slide into the water, the noise disappears. It's quiet in a way that feels mystical or holy. The reef below is covered in coral fans, schools of fish flickering like confetti as sunlight slices through the water in shifting beams. It's not the most colorful reef I've seen, but it's diverse and beautiful.

I float face down, breathing through the snorkel, and my whole body relaxes with the gentle bob of the waves.

Jamie grabs my hand underwater and squeezes, then points wildly ahead, nearly swallowing a mouthful of seawater. A turtle glides past, slow and unbothered, like it has nowhere else to be.

Jamie cries into her mask.

Later, Nina squeals through her snorkel when a school of tiny bright yellow fish swarms around her, and shortly after that, Tori spots a stingray burying itself in the sandy ocean floor.

Just as I think it couldn't possibly get any better, I notice something flash against the rocks while I'm drifting near a patch of coral.

At first, I think it's a shadow. Then it shifts, and my heart jumps. *Holy shit.* It's an octopus. I've never seen one in real life before, and I wonder if I'm making it up. I hover, holding myself still, watching as it unfurls two of its legs, skin rippling in gradients.

I lift my head out of the water and wave frantically at my friends, pointing and making muffled noises into my snorkel, but they look over too late. The octopus has already tucked back into hiding.

When we climb back onto the boat, I'm buzzing.

"What were you trying to show us?" Tori asks.

"An octopus!" I blurt.

Jamie gasps. "No way!"

I'm so excited, I don't even care that my face feels like it's been put through a juicer.

Ben overhears and grins. "Lucky." He hands in his fins and sits next to me.

The next snorkeling location isn't nearly as good as the first, so we spend most of our time on the beach. The guys find a spot to cliff jump, and we decide to join them. By the time we eat lunch and swim, it's time to get back on the boat and head to the ship.

Still no time for a complete debrief, but we did chat a little while wading in the shallows. It was enough time to tell them about the movie and the room service, but I don't quite get to the men's meeting or the massage and breakfast this morning.

They'd both take more explanation, and the setting isn't quite right for that.

We get back to the ship around three, sun-warmed, salty, and happy. The atrium is its usual chaotic elegance. Gleaming floors, the huge chandelier catching light, people spilling in from excursions with bags and souvenirs and sunburns.

We linger near the center, still talking and laughing with our group. Ben and his friends are fun. A bit immature, definitely younger than us, but that makes for a good hang on a beach day.

I'm half listening to Kipp recount his encounter with a four-foot-long—*his words*—barracuda when a specific head of hair moving through the crowd catches my attention.

Mason.

He's walking through the atrium in a cream linen button-up with Derek at his side, and it suddenly feels like I have a hummingbird trapped in my ribcage.

Mason's gaze finds me, and he pauses midsentence. His face softens, and then he says something to Derek before walking over.

The conversation around me blurs, and I'm suddenly hyper-aware of my wet hair, my sun-reddened cheeks, and the fact that I probably smell like sweat and sunscreen.

"Hey." Mason stops in front of me.

"Hey."

"How was your day?"

"Really gr—" I start, then jolt when Ben swings an arm over my shoulder.

"She was the only one to see an octopus," he says, his hand squeezing my arm.

Mason's jaw tightens. "Wow. That's something." His eyes flick down to the arm draped across me, then back up to my face.

"It was very cool." I shift slightly so Ben's arm naturally slides off.

Ben grins, unfazed. "We're all doing singles dinner tonight. You going?" He tips his chin to look down at my face.

"We got our matches!" Jamie thrusts her phone in front of me.

Matches? I have no idea what she's talking about.

"Our dates. For the different dinner courses and the salsa lesson. It's on the app."

Ben pulls his phone out, as do the rest of the people in our group besides Chloe, who still refuses to walk around with her phone on the ship.

My brain is blank, and my face is definitely showing it.

"Did you not fill out your survey?" Jamie lowers her phone.

My stomach drops. *Survey.* I remember the little notification on the app after the mixer and speed dating.

I remember thinking, *I'll do it later,* and then everything with Mason and my head and him being sick. The survey slid into the abyss of things I pushed off in favor of massages and room service.

I pull out my phone and check the app.

"Yep, I've got mine," Nina announces.

Ben and his friends are looking at their phones and seem to be happy with what they find, but me? No match. No notification. No assigned dinner date.

I slide my phone back into my purse. "Bummer. Guess I can't go."

Derek, still standing there with Mason, scoffs. "Fill it out now. There are plenty of people who didn't do theirs. I'm about to send out a reminder with a new link."

"Okay. Cool. I'll get on that." My eyes flick to Mason, communicating what I hope he interprets as "please make sure my link gets lost."

His lip quirks, then he shifts his attention to the group. "See you all at dinner." As he turns and walks away with Derek, my lungs deflate. It's like I'd been unplugged all day, and the second I was in his vicinity, my batteries began to charge.

Jamie grips my arm so hard, I wince. "What was that?"

"Ow! What was—"

"You're coming with me. Now."

Jamie treats me like I'm a raccoon with its paws in the trash, marching me out of the room. As soon as Chloe, Tori, and Nina catch sight of what's happening, they bolt away from Ben's group and follow us to the elevators.

Chloe blows out a breath as we wait for the doors to open. "Damn. And here I was getting worried we'd leave without an intervention."

"This isn't—" I try to yank my arm from Jamie's grip, but she's got it locked. We ride to deck five and squish into Jamie and Chloe's cabin.

All of us are still damp from snorkeling. My hair is so full of salt that it could probably do that Something About Mary thing, and my cover-up is sticking to my thighs.

"Sit," Jamie commands.

I shiver in the air-conditioned cold. "We could shower—"

"Nope." Jamie blocks the door, and we all pile onto the beds. When we're settled, our arms and legs sprawling over each other, she says, "Start talking."

I play at innocence, but the truth is, I've been dying to

come clean all day. I don't want to tell them, but I absolutely want to tell them. And that's why you need good friends who won't give you the option to be chicken shit.

The floodgates burst. "Mason's not a paramedic. He's a therapist. He's working with Dreamboat to help build their singles program, and there was this meeting with the guys where they talked about connection and not being afraid, and I went because Mason was completely passed out—that's when I saw him, you know. He was super sick, and you guys, he has a killer body. Not a gym-rat body, just a nice one. He's long and lean with nice skin, and he was cold so I kind of cuddled him, but then we were stuck in the room all day, and he felt terrible about it, so he gave me a massage, and—"

"WHOA." Tori holds up both her hands. "I'm going to need you to take those one at a time, please."

I suck in a breath and try to calm my racing heart.

Chloe clicks her tongue. "You can start with Mason's body. If you want."

I start there, surprised at how much I have to say about it, then take my time with the rest, and after a lengthy discussion about the men's meeting, I finally end with our breakfast that morning. Then I feel guilty for making everything about me and try to ask them about everything they did in Key West, but they refuse to bite.

Nina flips her hair. "We can talk about that at dinner when other people are present. I want to know why you didn't do something after that massage."

My throat thickens. "Because. It wasn't like that."

"Girl." Chloe purses her lips. "It was definitely like that."

"He was being nice." It's not the right way to describe it. It wasn't just 'nice.' It was *right*. When they all burst out laughing, I can't help but grin. "You don't get it!" I argue. "He's just —I don't know. It feels deep or something. Our conversations. You know?"

Tori crosses her arms over her chest. "You have feelings for him."

"I don't—" I start, then stop because lying in front of these women is like trying to hide a bonfire with a napkin. "I like him. Yes. He's a great guy. But you can't 'have feelings' after three days."

Tori tilts her head. "Why not? I mean, think about it. If you go on ten dates with someone, that would be what, twenty to thirty hours? You've just spent more than that with him."

I want to argue, but she makes an excellent point. It takes me a minute to come up with something. "This is a cruise, though. Not real life. It's a bubble."

"So? Why not lean into it?" Jamie asks. "What's the worst that could happen?"

My eyes widen. "The worst that could happen? I have to room with him for the rest of the trip, first of all. Second, if—" I stop myself. The words I'd typically say about not wanting to get involved with someone when it will probably end badly or get messy die on my tongue.

This wouldn't get messy. And it can't end badly because on Saturday, we're all getting off of this ship and going our own directions. I would never have to see him again.

"It's not what I want," I say, my voice low.

"Mason?" Jamie asks.

I shake my head. "No. Some fling. It sounds fun, but . . ." I shake my head, my heart speeding again. I don't want to do anything with Mason because I know Tori's right. I do have feelings for him. I like the questions he asks. I like how he makes me feel. And that scares the hell out of me because those feelings may as well be foreign currency.

I don't know how to do the exchange, and if I switch over? If I let myself live in that world where a man listens to me, compliments me, and does thoughtful things for me? I can't think of anything worse for my mental health than knowing a man like that exists when I have no chance of keeping him.

Chloe picks at a nail. "What if it's not a fling?"

I open my mouth.

Close it.

She continues, "When I was fourteen, there was this guy at summer camp. His name was Trent. He was tall, he had freckles, and he won the canoe races every time. Once, he gave me half his peanut butter sandwich. I never kissed him because he lived forty-five minutes away from me, and I thought we'd never see each other when we went home. I still regret it."

Tori laughs, and Chloe looks up. "You think I'm joking, but I'm serious. I've always wondered what would've happened."

Jamie leans forward. "That's legit good advice, though. Maybe stop thinking about whether it's practical and ask if you'll regret it instead. If it can't go anywhere, then maybe you tell him."

I frown. "Tell him what?"

"Everything you're feeling!" Jamie throws up her hands. "Like, maybe on the last day or something so it won't be awkward, but when do you get to be honest with a guy with zero consequences? You don't have to play the game because you'll never see him again."

Nina nods. "Yeah. You don't have to plan the wedding, but maybe stop acting like you're above wanting someone."

I cough a laugh. "I'm not above it!"

Chloe makes a noise. "You totally are. Ever since hockey boy."

"Okay, that's not fair. It's only been six months."

Chloe doubles down. "You're one awkward dinner away from joining a convent."

It seems like I'm not the only one who finds that mental image hilarious because we all devolve into laughter.

"You got what you wanted, okay? I have to shower." I try to push up from the bed, but Nina pulls me back down.

She presses my head to her chest. "I want you to record it. When you tell Mason you want to—"

"Thank you, Nina. I'll take that into consideration." I laugh and slip out from under her arm. "And now I must shower." I wait for Jamie to give me the okay, then bolt to the door.

"Maybe Mason's back in the room!" she says as I turn the handle.

I shush her. "If he is, I don't want him hearing any of this." I flash a pleading smile.

"He's not! There's the women's meeting before dinner, right?" Chloe says.

My eyes widen. I completely forgot. "Meet out here in thirty?"

Jamie shakes her head. "Forty-five. We can be fashionably late."

As Chloe predicted, Mason isn't in the cabin when I enter, and I'm beyond grateful. I'm not a good actress, and I need a little time to compose myself and not look like I was just talking about his body with all my girlfriends.

I stand under the shower and let the water run over my head, hoping my brain will stop buzzing. No dice.

I picture Mason in the atrium, jaw tightening when Ben threw an arm around me. I picture his eyes flicking to my face. I picture his hands and what I know they feel like.

I wash and rinse, then spend extra time conditioning and using the travel skincare products I always pack for vacation but never actually use.

I pick a plum colored dress that skims my body, smooth lotion over my legs, and curl my hair into loose waves.

My phone buzzes as I'm fastening my bracelet. It's an app notification for my survey link. I tap it open and look at the first question. It's multiple choice, and I wonder how they're using our answers to match with other people. Then I wonder if Mason filled it out. If there's a way for me to answer so I'll be paired with him?

I click 'C' and move on to question two. *Here goes nothing.*

Chapter Fourteen

We're only five minutes late to the meeting, and it's just as good as the men's. Possibly better because Mason's running it. He admits to everyone what his goal was on the ship and why he's there. He asks incredible questions. *What makes you feel safe enough to open up? When do you feel most wanted?* We talk about how men need to feel useful, how women need to feel seen, and I try to engage while fighting off the feeling that I wish it were only me and him in this room.

I thought I wasn't a selfish person. But I'm struggling to want to share.

Mason is swarmed at the end of the meeting, and it makes me so itchy, I suggest we go up to dinner early.

The dining room is stunning. Soft lighting. White tablecloths. Little flickering candles with golden light that makes everyone look ten percent hotter. The ship started moving again during my shower, and it must be a little choppy out because I'm aware of the sway. Not nerve-racking at all.

I step inside with Jamie, Chloe, Tori, and Nina to find that most of the men are already seated at tables marked with numbers. My assignments showed up at the beginning of the meeting.

After chatting for a bit, I scan the room for my first table number and see the other women arriving. Mason enters with them and walks straight to his table.

I check the number. Not mine.

He's in a navy button-down, his sleeves rolled, and a woman in a red dress lights up as he stops in front of her.

She smiles, and greets him with a hug, then says something that Mason listens to, his mouth curving into an easy smile.

Something hot and sharp sears my middle, and the evidence from the last few hours starts to stack up.

Okay.

So maybe I did have more than a few feelings for him.

I tear my eyes away and follow the host to my first table. I barely register the man's name before he launches into a story about his startup. Something with apps. Or coins. Or apps that are also coins?

I nod at appropriate intervals, laugh politely, and definitely don't notice how Mason's head tips back in laughter across the room.

Between courses, I find Tori and get a debrief of her first pairing. She looks a little flushed, and while it could be the wine, the twinkle in her eye says otherwise.

"You don't have to plan the wedding," I tease. She rolls her eyes and walks toward her next assigned table.

Once I find my own table, I only have to wait thirty seconds to learn that my main-dish pairing is with Ben.

He slides into the seat across from me, all confidence and easy charm. "Well, you clean up nice."

I smile. He looks good with product in his hair and a white Polo shirt. "Hi, Ben."

"I knew we were compatible." He leans back in his chair. "I love Octopuss-es."

I purse my lips. "Wow. We're doing that?"

He laughs. "C'mon. It was funny."

"How drunk are you?"

He gives me a look. "Do you really think it takes alcohol for me to make a joke like that?"

I laugh. Fair point.

He talks easily. About the snorkeling. About his life back home. I find out he's taking over his dad's construction business, and I'm honestly interested when he explains the logistics of modernizing a company built in the early 2000s.

He's fun to talk to, and he seems genuinely curious about what I do as a physical therapist. Still. I can't help but notice Mason. He's like my phone sitting on the counter. I keep catching that color of blue in my periphery and thinking I have a notification.

I didn't think I was a jealous person.

This dinner and the meeting before has proven me wrong.

Ben clears his throat. "So. What are you looking for?"

I blink. "What?"

"With this whole singles thing. Fun?"

I explain the situation with Jamie and her birthday celebration, then ask him the same question.

His answer surprises me. "Just wanted to go on real dates, I guess. Maybe we make this all too serious. It's fun to be with someone new. Talk. You know?"

My heart twinges. No, I didn't know. Not until he just said that. Was it possible to go out with someone and talk? Have fun? Not worry about expectations or what it all meant? "That's what people used to do," I say. "Barn dances and community dinners."

Ben lights up. "Right? It wasn't a big deal. Just ask someone to spend the night on your arm."

I glance up, and my heart skips a beat. Mason's watching

me. For half a second, the noise fades. He doesn't smile. Doesn't wave.

Then Ben says something else, and the moment breaks.

We're ushered to our next tables for dessert, and by the time I finish my chocolate layer cake, and they're announcing the salsa dancing, I'm exhausted.

The snorkeling, time in the sun, talking with my friends, and then working my ass off to engage all night and not look like I was staring at Mason. All of it makes me want to crawl into bed and sack out.

Plus, the idea of watching Mason holding someone else sounds like my personal hell at the moment. I don't know why I'm reacting so strongly, and it scares me.

I stand, slip my purse onto my shoulder, thank my date, and step away from the table.

I only make it three steps.

"Liv."

That voice stops me cold.

I turn, and Mason's there. Standing close enough, I can smell his cologne that still lingered in the bathroom when I was getting ready.

"You leaving?" he asks.

"I was thinking about it."

He glances toward the dance floor, where couples are already gathering. Then back at me.

"Dance with me?"

Chapter Fifteen

I don't dance.

I'm reminded of that fact the second we reach the dance floor, and Mason takes my hand.

"I should've said no," I whisper.

Mason's brow dips. "Why?"

"Because I can't dance."

"Who told you that?" he asks, and I laugh out of sheer surprise.

"How do you always do that?"

Mason grins, pulling me into what I assume is a proper dancing hold, his hand lifting mine. I drop my other hand on his arm as he finds my waist. "Do what?"

"Say things I don't expect."

Mason moves side to side, and I try to follow. "If you'd said you don't know how to dance, I would've believed you. But you said you *can't*. That's not something you'd tell yourself unless someone else said it first."

He's right. A memory flashes in my head. Third grade. I was in the elementary choir, and they wanted to do a section with light choreography. We all learned the dance. Then half of us were asked to stand in a line behind the others and not do the actions. To make it look better.

My breath quickens, my body realizing what's happening before I do. "I don't want to want you," I say, discovering my truth as it leaves my mouth.

His brows lift. It takes him a moment to compose himself, and that hesitation makes heat flood my core.

"Well. We don't always get what we want."

I laugh out loud, and when I recover, I swear Mason pulls me a little closer than I was before. "Don't make light of this. It's a real problem."

"Okay." He smirks.

"I barely know you."

"Right."

"And I'm not someone who does flings. They're not good for women anyway. The men looking for that are always assholes."

"I agree."

"Of course you do," I murmur, blowing out a breath.

Mason's hand shifts on my lower back. We're not moving at all to the beat, just swaying side to side, but at least I can handle that.

"Did you get in some good research? At dinner?" I try to change the subject since I have no idea what to say next.

"Is that what you want to talk about?"

I tip my chin and look up at him. "No."

The song ends. Applause ripples around us.

Mason stops moving. "Do you want to keep dancing?" I shake my head, and his throat bobs. "What do you want?"

I wet my lips. "I want to live in a world where I don't have consequences."

This time, Mason laughs out loud. "For what?"

I rest against his shoulder, tilting my mouth to his ear so nobody else can hear us. "You know what. I want to sleep with you. But I also know that's a terrible decision. Either it will be amazing, and I'll be ruined when I go back home and never see you again, or it will be awkward because I'll say that out loud, and you won't want to. Too late on that one, I guess. Then we have to share the same room for the rest of the week." I sigh. "See? Too complicated. I don't want to want it."

I pull back and motion at the gorgeous dining room around us. "This is the problem with all of this. It makes me want. And I was perfectly happy at home."

Mason sets my hand on his shoulder and loops his other arm around my waist as a new song starts up. "Okay, you named two risks. Emotional loss if it's meaningful, and emotional discomfort if it's rejected. Both of those are about vulnerability, not sex. And wanting now doesn't mean you were unhappy before. It means a new life experience exposed a need you forgot you had. Because you've lived without it for so long."

The corners of my eyes prick. Damn, he's good. "That's not fair."

A laugh rumbles in his chest. "I know. Sorry."

"Do you do this to all your friends?"

He sighs. "Unfortunately. Yes."

Jamie walks by, giving me a long look, and I blink. I'd forgotten we were in a public place. "So what do I do, oh wise one?" I tease. It's not lost on me that he hasn't responded to my almost question about whether he's interested. Whether he'd say yes to what I wanted if I honestly asked.

Mason considers. "You want vulnerability, but the consequences of sex scare you." He taps his finger against my hip. "There are plenty of ways to physically connect without it."

I can barely feel my fingers. "Like?"

He meets my eyes, his long lashes shadowing his cheeks. "Come on."

I let him lead me off the floor, past the tables, past my friends who watch us go with identical expressions of glee. My heart kicks like a bass drum as Mason's fingers tighten around mine, and we walk toward the exit.

Mason swipes his wristband, then moves to the side so I can enter our room first. When the door clicks behind me, my ears start to ring.

I stand there, arms wrapped around myself, completely exposed without having taken off a single stitch of clothing.

I can't believe I said that to him. I can't believe I told him exactly what I was thinking, and it didn't freak him out at all.

Every second with Mason feels easy. New and terrifying, but seamless. No games, no pretending. I'm worried I'm already addicted.

Mason walks in, and we both slip off our shoes.

"That color looks great on you," he says.

I bite my lip. "Not helping."

He grins, adjusts the waistband of his pants, then turns to me. We're only a foot apart since there's barely walking space between the end of the bed and the desk. He takes a step forward and lifts a hand, pausing before he touches me.

"Is this okay?" he asks.

I nod.

He rests his palm on my forearm. The contact is so simple,

it makes me dizzy. "This is what people forget," he murmurs. "Humans need touch. It's not optional."

His thumb moves once, like punctuation. "When babies don't get held, they stop thriving. Literally, their bodies shut down. And elderly people, when they go too long without human contact, their health declines faster. Immune systems weaken. Depression spikes. Mortality rates go up."

I swallow, then reach my hand out, resting it on his hip.

He watches me. "Touch is regulation. It tells your nervous system you're not alone. That you're safe."

Every nerve in my body lights up. I've been touched before. Plenty. But it always feels like a prelude, a negotiation. An expectation. "I think . . . men only touch me when they want something."

He nods. "I believe that. We've all learned that bodies are only sexual."

"How do we unlearn that?" I whisper.

He drops his head, pressing his forehead to mine, and I suck in a breath. "I don't know. But I think it starts with curiosity. Intention."

I'm definitely curious. I could lift onto my toes and kiss him. I want to feel his mouth on mine so bad it aches.

Instead, I raise a palm to his cheek and push my fingers up into the hair just above his ears.

He brushes his lips over my temple. "When you were a kid, what did you want to be when you grew up?"

I close my eyes. "A veterinarian."

Mason smiles against my cheek. "You like animals?"

"Love them. But then I discovered I was allergic."

"To all of them?"

I shake my head. "Cats and dogs."

"So you could have a horse. Or a potbelly pig."

"Tempting."

"You gave up on your dream too early."

"Story of my life."

Mason flicks off the light, then tugs on my arm, leading me to the bed. We lie down together, and Mason pulls me into him, wrapping his arms around me and molding me to his body.

"Did you know there are professional cuddlers?" I say. "People pay for some stranger to come into their house and hold them." Before this trip, I would have mocked them so hard. In fact, I'm pretty sure I did on a phone call with Chloe.

Now? I think they might be geniuses.

Mason curls his arm so he can run his fingers through my hair. "Are you saying you're going to pay me?"

I laugh. "Depends. This is your job interview."

Mason plays with my hair, and I drag my fingernails over his arm in languid circles. I feel the bones in his wrist, feel the edges of his knuckles. I have no idea how much time has passed, but when I can't take it any longer, I rotate to face him, sliding my knee between his legs.

"Is kissing allowed? Or is that too much?" I can't see him in the dark, but his breath whispers over my forehead.

"I don't think that's too much." He smooths the hair from my face, then cups my jaw. "How do you like to be kissed?"

I work to catch my breath. His questions are like a jolt of adrenaline to my brain. "I don't know." That was the truth. Since high school, every time I'd kissed someone, it was always a stepping stone. Something to lead to an endpoint, not the destination in and of itself.

But what would it feel like if it were? I'm suddenly desperate to find out.

The tip of Mason's nose brushes mine, and his thumb rests under my chin. He presses a kiss to the corner of my mouth.

Had I ever paid attention to what that felt like before?

Lips touching my skin? My head was always too busy thinking about what came next, what I should be doing with my hands, or—

Another brush of his lips, and a ripple of energy rushes over my skin. I want to kiss him back, and I must move too fast because he smiles against my mouth.

"Sorry." My fingers curl at the base of his neck.

"Don't apologize. I liked that."

The words send a thrill through me. "How do you just tell the truth like that? It's seems so easy for you."

"Except when Derek tells everyone I'm a paramedic."

I breathe a laugh. "I mean, that lie was kind of obvious."

"I thought I pulled it off well."

"You didn't know what Narcan was."

It's his turn to laugh. "Damn my innocent questions."

I kiss him again, cataloguing everything. The way his lips tense and release, the tingle from his lip balm, the rush of his quickening breath.

His hand trails down my neck, resting over my collarbone, and my brain snaps between the two points of contact, then finds a third at our hips and can't decide which is most exciting to pay attention to.

It's complete sensory immersion. Like sinking into warm sand.

He shifts, pressing closer and angling his head, more of his mouth catching mine. His thumb brushes my jaw once, a soft sweep that sends a shiver down the length of my spine.

I taste him, running my tongue over his lower lip. Not because I'm supposed to or because I think it might turn him on, but because I want to. Because I'm curious.

He runs his hand over my shoulder, then follows the curve of my waist. My hip. "Your body is beautiful," he murmurs, and it's the first time a man has ever said that to me and it felt like a fact, not an ask.

I feel for the hem of his shirt and slide my hand over the flat of his stomach. *Touch is regulation.* I don't know why I say it, but the words, "You're safe," slip past my lips.

Mason sucks in a breath, his mouth hovering over mine. "I know." He kisses my cheek, my jaw, then nudges my head to the side and kisses down the length of my neck.

When he resurfaces, he pulls me flush against him, cradling my head and pulling me into the hollow of his shoulder.

My breathing shifts to match his. My heart somehow slowing to beat to the same rhythm it feels from his knocking through my skin.

I try to stay exactly in that moment. To quiet the thoughts swirling in my head. But my brain can't help but send up a warning bell.

Three days.

Ba-dump.

Ba-dump.

We only have three days.

Chapter Seventeen

At some point during the night, we brush our teeth and change out of our clothes. I sleep in Mason's arms, which I didn't believe was physically possible. Anytime I stayed the night with a man in the past, I had to have my own space. Room to breathe.

But waking up to an empty bed that morning felt wrong. I check and re-check my bag at least four times before meeting up with the girls because every time I try to leave, it feels like I'm missing something.

Tori notices something is different the second I show up at the breakfast buffet. She gives me a look, but neither of us says anything. It felt the same when she called with a positive pregnancy test.

There are some things you tease about and some things you don't. Some things take time to put into words, and I don't have the words for last night yet. It feels like the most beautiful secret, one that might slip through my fingers the second I let it out.

Three days.

"The fruit looks amazing today," Tori says.

I nod and take a huge scoop from the bowl.

I tuck all my thoughts away as we tube caves in Belize, and this time, Ben's group isn't with us. It's mystical and other-worldly. We laugh and reminisce, eat incredible stewed meat, rice and beans, and drink some nectar from the gods called Soursop.

When I return to the cabin after dinner, Mason's there, working. I briefly consider pulling out my laptop and answering work emails, but when he sees me, he closes his computer and sets his glasses on the nightstand.

"How was your day?"

I drop my bag and crawl into bed with him, curling up against his chest to tell him everything.

* * *

Two days.

The water off Dreamboat's private island is so clear it feels unreal, like someone turned the saturation on their phone up to a hundred percent.

I wade into the Caribbean barefoot, the sand cool and soft between my toes, the tide rolling in gentle waves that lap against my calves like a personal greeting. *Hello, old friend.*

I draw a deep breath, reveling in the hush of the tide and the music from steel drums drifting over from the beach. There's plenty going on behind me, but my eyes are locked straight ahead.

Mason's out in the water with a few guys from the Buoys and Girls events, Ben included. Apparently, while we were off caving yesterday, Mason held a series of workshops on the ship for those who weren't out on excursions. They were a massive hit, and now he's Mister Popular. No surprise there.

"This is it." Nina drops her bag on a lounge chair. "This is the highlight reel."

Jamie whoops and sprints straight for the water, throwing her cover-up onto the sand. Chloe shakes her head, already scanning for a shade umbrella to park under.

A guy approaches Mason in the waist-deep water, rubbing the back of his neck. Mason nods, says something, and the guy's shoulders visibly drop.

My chest swells. *This is who he is.* Not just with me. With the world. He's kind and helpful and real, and I don't know what the hell I'm going to do without it when we disembark tomorrow.

Twenty minutes later, Jamie slides in beside me, handing me a piña colada. "You look like you're watching an episode of Ted Lasso."

I laugh. "I think I kind of am."

She follows my gaze and grins. "You love him."

My eyes sting. "I've known him for less than a week."

"Yep."

I take a drink, letting the tiny flecks of ice melt over my tongue. "I'm an idiot."

"Maybe." She watches the scene with me for a moment. "Or maybe not."

The day unfolds in a blur of sun, warm water, fantastic food, and laughter. We kayak. We snorkel. At one point, Mason and I find ourselves waist-deep in the water, passing a ball back and forth with Jamie and Ben. The sun glints off the surface, bright enough to make my eyes water, and I feel . . . awake. Fully in my body. Maybe for the first time ever.

Ben tosses the ball, and I miss it. As I slog through the water to grab it, Mason barrels toward me with a goofy grin on his face.

"No!" I run faster, but he's already a foot closer than I am.

"It's mine!" I laugh as his hand brushes the ball, and I leap onto him, sending us both under the waves.

At the BBQ, I catch Jamie and Nina talking with Mason, and I walk the other way. One day left, I remind myself. But it feels important that they get to know him. If I have to share him during these last hours, I'd rather it be with them.

Back on the ship, the shift is palpable. Everyone buzzes with that end-of-vacation high where everything feels heightened and fleeting.

People naturally pair off for dinner that night, and based on what we observed on the beach, I'm not at all surprised that Ben sits next to Nina. Or that Luke finds a way to join the end of the table next to Tori.

I hate that Mason's wrapping things up with the management team.

Jamie clinks her glass and gives a toast. "This is the best birthday I've ever had." Her eyes shine. "Thank you for coming with me, and for being up for all of this even though I didn't tell you I signed us up."

We laugh and cry and eat, then go for round two. I prioritize my friends and don't bow out early even though it's killing me, wondering if Mason is back yet.

When I get to the room around one in the morning, my heart falls. Mason's asleep on the bed. One arm flung over his eyes. Hair mussed. Shirt rumpled.

One more day.

I move quietly, brushing my teeth and changing into pajamas, but he stirs when I sit on the edge of the bed.

"Hey," he murmurs, voice thick with sleep.

"Hey."

I slide under the covers and reach for him. We lie there in the dark, and I want to let him go back to sleep, but my thoughts from the beach and dinner are too loud to shut down.

"I'm scared," I whisper.

His hand shifts on my arm. "Of what?"

"Tomorrow. Going back to everything."

He exhales slowly. "Yeah. Me too."

"Where do you go next?"

"Back to New York. I'm staying with my brother."

I nod. "That will be nice." My throat thickens, making it hard to speak. *No*, I think. Not hard to speak. Hard not to say the things I'm too afraid to let out.

But it's the last night.

I think of Chloe and Jamie's words. Not what should I do, but what would I regret not doing?

Even if Mason and I can't be a thing, even if this has just been a vacation bubble and none of it would survive in the real world, I know with a surety that I'd regret not saying what I feel. He needs to know how much this week has changed my life. Has changed me.

I wet my lips. "I love this week. I love that we got stuck in a cabin together." I pause to catch my breath, my heart racing. "I love everything you taught me, and I love—" My voice catches. "I love you, Mason. I know our lives are far apart, and those feelings might not be the same for you because you're amazing at connection and talking to people, but I need you to know that."

The silence is all-consuming when I stop talking.

That confession was a choice. Something I wanted to tell him. I don't expect anything in return, but I can't pretend I don't want it. I want to know that what happened here, all the time we spent together, mattered to him, too.

"I am good at talking to people," he says. "But that doesn't mean it isn't hard work."

I frown, not sure where he's going with that.

His thumb brushes my jaw. "With you, it doesn't feel like work."

My heart warms. I curl my fingers in his shirt, but before I can get comfortable, Mason rolls back and hits the lamp on the nightstand. I blink, wincing at the light.

"Sorry. I want to look at you when I say this." He rolls closer, shifting so our faces are in line. His eyes travel to my brow, my cheek, my lips, then back to my eyes. "I love you, too." He smiles to himself, pushing a loose tendril of hair from my cheek. "They gave me an option to move."

I blink. "Move where?"

His grin widens. "Cabins. Derek called corporate and explained the situation. I guess he felt bad when he saw how mad you were."

I laugh. "I wasn't mean, was I?"

Mason shakes his head. "No. Just a little spicy. I liked it."

"When did he tell you that?"

"That night."

I push up to my elbow. "The first night? You knew before the mixer?"

He shakes his head. "After." His tongue flicks over his lower lip. "But I saw you in that room talking to your friends, and I knew if I switched, I wouldn't have an excuse to talk to you again."

I raise an eyebrow. "You chose to room with me."

His jaw works. "I did. And Derek didn't say anything since this is a work trip and I really shouldn't be hooking up with the clientele."

I laugh. "But we didn't hook up."

Mason's eyes glint. "I know. What we did was so much worse."

My face softens. "So much worse."

He kisses me then. Deep and slow. And I know in that instant that there's one more thing I'll absolutely regret not doing.

I pull back and search those beautiful green eyes. "I want more than just touch tonight."

He slow blinks, and it sends a jolt between my thighs. "I don't want to hurt you."

I nod. "I know. I think it's too late for that."

He kisses my cheek, and I tug at his shirt.

One more day.

I wake with Mason's arm heavy across my waist and the steady hum of the ship under the mattress. His breathing is slow and even, and for a few seconds, I let myself pretend we're not on a floating hotel that's about to spit us back into real life.

My phone buzzes on the nightstand. I can barely reach it with my left hand.

JAMIE:

> Heading to the buffet. Don't you dare
> look cute

I smile into the pillow, then carefully slide out from under Mason's arm.

He makes a sound, then turns his head. "Where are you going?"

"Go back to sleep. I'm meeting up with the girls for breakfast." I plant a kiss on his forehead, and his hand brushes up my arm.

Somehow, I have the self-control to pull on a hoodie and joggers. I pause at the door and look back at him. His eyes are closed, hair messy, his clothes still piled next to the bed where we left them last night.

I could climb back into bed. I know my friends would understand.

But I don't.

I made a promise to myself that I'd show up for my friends. And, annoyingly, Mason isn't the kind of guy who'd appreciate me breaking it.

The buffet is quieter than it's been all week. People move slower, and the staff are already starting to prepare for the next week of guests.

Jamie wears an oversized sweater with her hair in a messy bun and sunglasses on indoors like she's a celebrity avoiding paparazzi. As I approach, she holds up a hand. "I already cried once this morning. Let me eat my feelings before you say anything."

The five of us fill our plates and sit down in a corner booth. It doesn't take long for the gossip to come out.

"Nina slept with Ben," Chloe says as she takes a bite of eggs Benedict.

Jamie gasps. "What?! I'm shocked!"

Nina chortles. "Okay, stop. Tori and Luke—"

"Okay, okay." Tori blushes. "We don't need to talk about it."

"Uh, yes. We do." Jamie leans in, then stops when she realizes Chloe is staring at me.

"What?" I drop my eyes to my plate and scoop up a forkful of scrambled eggs.

"Oddly silent this morning," Chloe says.

I scoff. "Jamie said not to talk until she ate. You're all going to make her cry again."

Tori squints. "You do look rather peaceful."

"I slept well," I say, but I can't pretend for a second longer. "Because I slept with Mason."

The table erupts.

"Freaking finally!" Jamie crows, and the elderly couple across from us gives us all dirty looks.

I lower my voice. "You can't say that when it's only been a week!"

The conversation devolves from there, and we talk about all of it. We even get some juicy details out of Tori, which is our most impressive accomplishment.

We spend the late morning wandering the ship, taking stupid photos, pretending to be Jack and Rose off the back of the ship. The usual, which we then spam to Mel's phone.

At one point, we end up on a quiet stretch of deck chairs by the empty running track, the sun warming our legs, the breeze tugging at our hair. We talk for what feels like hours, the sea rolling by beside us like a screen saver.

Turns out, it isn't just me who realizes they're a little lonely back at home. And it isn't just because we aren't paired up with significant others. We need more of this. More connection, as Mason said.

We brainstorm how we could create that without moving to a commune in South America, though all of us agree that's also a tempting option.

I question everything about my life. My job. My house. My routines.

What if it looked different?

It's scary and exhilarating, and makes it obvious which things I want—like my patients—and which things I could get rid of. Basically, everything else.

When it's time to hit the lunch buffet, even though none of us have felt hunger in a week, I hold my friends back for a second and pull them into as much of a circle as I can with the chairs in the way. "I love you," I say. "Like, really love you. I hope you know that if you need anything, I'm always there for you, and—" my voice catches. "I'm so glad we met at the boxing studio and that you all put in effort so we can stay friends—"

I start to cry to a chorus of "I love you, too!"

We hug. Then eat our obligatory pound of pasta and cake.

We sit by the pool in the afternoon and watch a movie in the theater. Mason texts me on the app letting me know he'll be done at four. There's a themed party and farewell mixer, but I'm not going to that. My friends do, in fact, completely understand.

When I open the door to our room, Mason is inside, putting something into his suitcase. He turns, then drops the folded clothing with a smile. "Hi."

I rush forward and kiss him.

No more days.

Chapter Nineteen

Even after an hour in bed together, my packing isn't efficient. It's slow and distracted. We can't stop talking, trying to get out an entire life's worth of thoughts in the minutes we have left.

We trade stories about our worst vacations. Childhood memories. High school. College. First jobs, first loves. We order room service and eat in bed. When he drops a fry and tries to save it before ketchup hits the comforter, I laugh so hard, I cry.

And then I cry for real.

Mason sets his plate on the counter and holds me.

We don't solve it because we can't, but we do talk about logistics. You know. Because it's fun to rationally confirm there's no way we could ever be together.

"I'd have to leave Montana," I whisper.

"I would never ask you to do that."

"You can't stop traveling."

He exhales. "It's not that I can't."

"But you're passionate about your work."

He nods. That was the truth. Mason is easy to love. And he also loves a lot of things. I'm only lucky to be one of them.

"What time do you leave the ship?" he asks.

"Nine-thirty."

"And then you're off to the airport?"

I nod. "My flight's at one." I draw a heavy breath. "Do you leave first thing?"

"I have a debrief at seven. Then there's staff changeover and some submissions I need to make."

Another wave of grief washes over me, and I bury my head in his chest. "I don't think I can handle saying goodbye."

Mason kisses my shoulder. "Okay. What do you want me to do?"

I hate myself for saying it, but the idea of watching him walk out the door makes me want to throw up. "Can you leave before I wake up?"

"Of course."

"I'm sorry."

"Don't be."

My tears soak into his shirt. "And then you have my number."

"I do."

I don't ask him to call, even though, of course, I want him to. I want to be the person who believes that love will find a way, that somehow we'll overcome every obstacle in our path to be together. But if Mason's taught me anything, it's that I'm happier when I tell the truth.

"Being together would take a lot of risk," I say. "And I'm scared that I'm not the kind of person who can do that." Maybe that means that I'll never be able to have something like this, which is honestly terrifying. But leaving the life I know? Changing everything for something I don't know will work out? That's equally so.

"I'm scared that after all my work on connection and relationships, I'm too selfish to settle down," he says.

"You're not selfish."

He exhales. "I am, though. I like feeling important when I travel. I like new experiences. I like doing what I want. I like . . ." He swallows hard. "Being in control. And you make me feel very not in control."

I sniff. "Thanks. I'm glad I'm the better person in this relationship."

Mason laughs, then squeezes me tighter. "Let's get ready for bed."

We stack our plates outside the door, then go through the routine we've built together over the past week. I fold my life back into my suitcase like it didn't just expand into something so much bigger and set it in the hall.

Our plates are already gone.

* * *

When I wake up, the cabin is quiet.

The other side of the bed is cold.

There's a note on the nightstand, folded once, my name written in neat, careful letters. My chest caves in, and I cry so hard my body shakes.

Eventually, I force myself to stand. Shower. Dress.

I'm running late, so I tuck the note in my backpack to read at the airport and meet my friends in the hallway. It's comforting that their eyes are puffy, too. At least it's not just me.

The ship's final announcements echo overhead, and Jamie hugs me tight. "We'll do it again."

"I know," I whisper.

We walk off the ship together and, when it's our turn, collect our luggage. Our Uber takes us to the airport, and we get lunch together before we dash off to our different gates.

And then I'm alone.

I sit in the bucket seat and open my laptop. At least there are plenty of patient emails to keep me company.

Boarding goes smoothly, but the plane is freezing cold, reminding me that's the kind of temperature I have to look forward to back home. I slide into my window seat and tuck my backpack under the seat in front of me.

I pull up a book on my phone. It's a romance.

I try to play Bejeweled instead, but I can't focus on the lines, so I turn to the window and stare at the movement on the tarmac.

Tears blur my vision, and I swipe at my cheeks when there's movement behind me in the aisle. Not that I expected the middle seat to stay open, but one can hope.

"Is this seat taken?" a man's voice asks.

I freeze.

The guy sitting on the aisle says, "That's not how it works, bud. You have to sit where—"

"No, I know. It was—I was trying to make a joke."

I spin and look up, not able to compute the face looking back at me. "Mason?"

He holds up the boarding pass on his phone, tilting it toward the man below him as he mutters, "I feel like it's not funny if I have to say it again," then clears his throat. "Excuse me, Miss. Is this seat taken?"

Mason drops into the seat next to me, and I'm still speechless.

His mouth turns up at one corner. "Wow. Guess you really didn't expect my meetings to run on time."

I put my hand on his cheek to make sure he's real. *"What the hell are you talking about?"*

Mason blinks. "Didn't you read my note?"

Holy shit. The note.

I dive for my backpack and pull it out of the zipper sleeve, then flip it open.

Liv,

Couldn't sleep last night, so I did some research. Got in touch with an old contact early this morning. I knew he'd moved to a hospital in Montana, but I wasn't sure which. It's in Billings. So I changed my flight. Thought I'd come with you this afternoon if that works? There's a chance my meetings won't end on time, and I'll have to catch *the 4pm flight, but either way, I'll be there tonight. Zero pressure. But let's be clear. I'm not coming to Montana for the job.*

Love Mason

Tears stream over my cheeks when I look up. "I didn't read the note."

Mason's eyes are misty. "Well, sorry to—"

I grab his face and kiss him. "No pressure?" I hiss, attacking his mouth.

"I didn't want you to think—"

I nearly yank him into my seat. After another long drag, I allow him to pull back. "How did you get the seat next to me?"

"A very accommodating flight attendant."

"And how long will you stay?"

He pants. "Depends. It's a pilot program for young professionals experiencing burnout and isolation. If I'm a good fit, I'd be working for a few months there to help retention and life satisfaction."

I purse my lips. "Well, you better damn well be a good fit."

Mason laughs. "See? Spicy."

"Is your brother mad?"

"He's always mad. He's from Jersey."

I chortle, then brush my lips over his. "Do you want to stay with me?"

Mason watches me closely as he says his next words. "I booked a hotel. Not because I don't want to stay with you, because I do. But like you said, we met in a bubble. I don't want to put pressure on this. We should get to know each other there, too."

I nod. "But I think close quarters work for us."

He chuckles. "I only booked four nights."

"Perfect." I kiss him again. I can't stop kissing him. "But here's the deal. You will not tell any of my friends the truth about how this happened."

"Deal."

"The words *Buoys and Girls* will not be uttered in public."

He fights another laugh. "Maybe just if it comes up."

"No."

"If I'm saying 'boys and girls' and I massage the vowels a little—"

I groan and let go of his shirt. "And here we go. The guy who won't stop talking about the singles vacation we both didn't sign up for when his girlfriend asks him to. Such a cliché."

That time, the laugh wins, and Mason loses.

Epilogue

ONE YEAR LATER

Montana smells like rain. A storm is blowing in, and it's about damn time. We haven't had snow for over three weeks.

I'm barefoot in the kitchen, hair twisted up with a pencil because I can't find a hair tie, watching the pine trees shake in the wind while the coffee brews. Jamie starts singing at the top of her lungs in the living room just as Nina dances into the kitchen with her glass of orange juice that she insisted on pouring into a champagne glass, and Chloe and Tori are helping Mel get her luggage to the guest room.

It's Jamie's birthday again, and this time, we're all together stateside. Jamie fought hard for New York because she's been talking to Mason's brother off and on since they met at Christmas with us in Arizona. But, at seven months, I wasn't sure I should travel that far.

I drop my hand to my rounded stomach. What can I say? Mason and I like to move fast.

Tori's just grateful it wasn't her this time, though Ben swears he's working on it.

I step into the living room with a tray of mugs just as Mason comes in from outside with an armful of logs from the wood pile.

This is our house. That still gets me. We bought it six months ago. A modest place with a wraparound porch, a yard that borders on open space, and windows that face east in the morning. Mason says it was waiting for us, and I believe him.

He crosses the room and presses a kiss to my temple. "Feeling okay?"

I nod. "Great."

"Okay! Everybody listen up!" Jamie claps her hands together. When we're all paying attention, her eyes light up. "So I heard about a few things happening in Billings this weekend."

Groans echo around the room.

"Don't even!" She points first at the ring on Tori's finger and then to my stomach. "Clearly, this system works."

Mason wraps an arm around my waist and pulls me to his side as Jamie continues. "Are you sure you're feeling okay?"

"I think I just contracted gestational diabetes."

"Nope. You want dessert. What you need is preeclampsia. Requires bed rest."

"Perfect." I smack his butt and squeeze a little.

"Okay, Mason and Liv, I feel like you aren't paying atten-tion." Jamie points two fingers at us.

Mason stands straighter. "Right. Sorry." He winks at me because Jamie doesn't know yet that two can play at this game.

And his brother's showing up in an hour.

* * *

WATCH FOR BOOK 2: CABIN FEVER

About the Author

 Cindy Gunderson is a voice actress and award-winning author. Since she has commitment issues, she writes both sci-fi and fantasy, as well as contemporary romance and women's fiction under the pen name, Cynthia Gunderson.

When she is not typing away in a quiet corner of her local library, you can find her traveling with her family, narrating audiobooks, or happily digging in her garden. She loves acting and performing, beating her kids in card games, and playing ultimate frisbee with her handsome husband, Scott.

Cindy grew up in Alberta, Canada, but has lived most of her adult life between California and Colorado. She currently resides in the Denver metro area. Cindy holds a B.S. in Psychology from Brigham Young University.

Cindy's first novel Tier 1 was awarded First Place in Science Fiction at the 2021 CIPPA EVVY Awards and her women's fiction novel Yes, And was honored with the Indie Author Award's first place prize for the state of Colorado, 2023.

www.ingramcontent.com/pod-product-compliance
Lightning Source LLC
Chambersburg PA
CBHW040909010826
48978CB00013BB/1206